Song of
the Spirit

M. Lee Prescott

Published by Mt. Hope Press
Copyright 2014, Mt. Hope Press
Cover design by Lees River Studios
ISBN: 978-0-9912855-0-1

This book is a work of fiction. Names, characters, places, and events are products of the author's imagination or are used fictitiously. Any resemblance to actual people (alive or deceased), locales, or events is entirely coincidental.

For my children and grandchildren, with love and affection
for the history you create each day.

CHAPTER 1

Winnowing fingers of sunlight danced through the trees as the pair made their way through the forest. They'd been well-taught by their elders, taught to move like shadows through deep woods of silence. As they walked, scanning the ground, the older girl kept a watchful eye on her companion, never straying more than a few yards from her. It was the first year they'd been allowed to forage apart from the others and she recognized this freedom was also a test of her responsibility.

Suddenly the little one stopped, bending over to thrust her sharp, wooden tool into the earth, grunting as she struggled with the task. Immediately the older girl moved to her side. "Take care, little Dove. The roots are delicate and Na'go needs them whole. Don't cut too sharply with your dibble or there'll be nothing left of them."

She spoke softly, sensing that her words would be greeted with anger by the child, yet unable to stop herself. The roots of the red turnip—much scarcer than its white cousin and a favorite of their people—were too precious to end up in shreds. Harvested intact, the women could use them as the base of a delicious soup—perfect for the feasting in four days. In shreds, the root wouldn't last the night before rotting.

As the older girl watched, her sister's chubby hands worried the root, alternately pulling and chopping at it. Her face was all determination as she mined the tiny patch of tubers. "Go away, Wind Flower! I know how to do it. Na'go showed me!" she sputtered, her face the color of the root.

"I know little one. I just—

"And don't call me little one—my name is Laughing Dove!" she stammered, chin thrust out, eyes blazing up at her sister. "I'm not little, I'm not! Father says I'll be much taller than you when I'm grown."

Recognizing the futility of further conversation, Wind Flower wandered off a little, hoping albeit belatedly—to give her sister an unspoken message of trust. Glancing back she saw Laughing Dove's shoulders relax. She smiled, full of love for the seven-year-old—the only one of her siblings still alive. These days, life for the Cheyenne was full of sorrow, but out in the woods, away from the reservation and the soldiers' prying eyes, Wind Flower felt happy and free. Free as her people must have felt years ago. Before the coming of the Washita.

The soldiers had permitted this gathering for the renewal of the arrows and had not followed or pried into the sacred rite. They were busy elsewhere. Fighting still raged on the Plains and the army had little time for the ragged band of Cheyenne and Arapaho they had corralled onto the reservation. It was the year 1887 by the white man's reckoning and Wind Flower was thirteen.

Before her birth there had been Sand Creek, the massacre by the evil White Hair's army. The old ones still spoke of Black Kettle and White Hair who was killed at Greasy Grass. Wind Flower, two at the time of Greasy Grass, had often listened to whispered words of the battle the Washita called Little Big Horn. Whispered words of the man Custer and his defeat, hushed remembrances of a life that had all but vanished for the Cheyenne. The reservation on the Tongue River was the only home Wind Flower remembered. Still she longed for the past her parents spoke of now in sorrowful whispers, late at night while their children slept.

When Wind Flower was small, Little Wolf had led the people to the Tongue River. Since then the tribe had lived peaceably with their white jailers, but stories drifted back from the Plains where the Sioux fought on.

Of the journey to Tongue River, Wind Flower remembered little save the intense cold and the wailing that seemed to envelope the tribe, blanketing them in sorrow and grief. The Great Spirits took her two brothers before the march began, and another sister, Pale Deer, died during the winter spent in the frozen caves of Lost Chokeberry Creek.

Over the years, Wind Flower had heard many stories of the events that led the Cheyenne to the land of the Tongue. Stories of the surrender at Fort Robinson with Crazy Horse and many of his Ogalala Sioux with them. Stories of the Washita's betrayal and breaking of the treaty agreement, a betrayal that sent them to live in sickness and squalor with their Southern Cheyenne brothers. Stories telling of the fevers, chills and aching of the bones that had taken her brothers and many more until Little Wolf dared to break away and push northward. Now, they lived under the white man's thumb, caged like animals but in relative peace, with less sickness and death than there'd been in the South.

"Someday," said Na'go, her mother. "Someday, we may be able to wrench the fire water from the hands of our warriors and their strength will return. Then we can break away to live in freedom once more." Na'go sighed when she spoke, knowing the elusive nature of freedom now that the Washita were here to stay.

Finding another patch of turnip, not the sweet red turnip, but its more plentiful cousin, Wind Flower stooped and sunk her dibble into the surrounding earth, teasing the large, white roots out. She worked the smooth wooden spade carefully, shaking the dirt from unblemished roots as she tucked them into her bag before moving on. Thus they continued until the sun reached its uppermost point. It was Laughing Dove that began complaining.

Dove, so like their mother with her dark eyes, long braids, and chubby figure, had trudged along behind her older sister puffing noisily as the sun grew hotter, but now she'd reached her limit. There was no help for it. They would have to stop and rest, at least for a little while.

"Flower, I can't walk anymore," she whimpered, her voice echoing through the silence of the forest. The others were out of sight and hearing. To Dove, the woods, so cool and welcoming when they'd started out, now seemed full of unseen terrors.

Laughing Dove was afraid of everything, even the Wise Ones. Her sister knew she would soon be crying, imagining wild beasts all around them. "All right my sister, we'll stop, but only for a little while." They'd reached a clearing and Wind Flower set down her bag on the soft moss at the edge of the path, beckoning to her sister. "Come sit beside me and I'll sing."

As an infant, Laughing Dove had napped little and cried incessantly, no matter who held and coddled her. She would drink quietly at her mother's breast but the rest of the time she howled. One day when her na'go was too busy to hold her, she was handed to her elder sister.

Wind Flower took the tiny squalling baby and walked to the edge of camp, singing and rocking her. Round and plump even then, Laughing Dove's chubby, soft arms and tiny hands poked out of the blanket reaching up to her sister's braids. Wind Flower continued singing and rocking and before long the baby quieted. The perpetual crying had ceased as Laughing Dove lay gazing adoringly at her sister.

Wind Flower's singing had always been a source of cruel teasing among her people. While the other women's voices reached to the skies, her voice sank to the earth, like a stone dropping from a high cliff. Before that morning, Na'go would motion for silence whenever her eldest daughter burst into song, but never again. As long as she held her tiny sister, Wind Flower was never silenced.

To this day, Laughing Dove could always be comforted by her sister's songs and Wind Flower's kindred were forever grateful. A croaking girl's songs were always preferable to the screams of an unhappy child. Wind Flower felt needed. Upon her little sister, she could pour all the love she felt, all the love that her kindred had no time for anymore. As their world disappeared, wrenched away by the avarice of the Washita, her parents and elders had closed their hearts. Survival consumed every waking moment; there was no time for love.

The warm sunlight filtering down through the trees and her sister's singing lulled Laughing Dove to sleep. As her sister's breathing became regular, Wind

Flower leaned down to kiss her cheek, brushing damp curls from her face. Perhaps Dove should have stayed behind, she mused, thinking of the long walk ahead of them. Back to the camp with over two hundred tipis arched in a huge crescent, curving towards the mountains beyond the plain. "Sleep my little one," she whispered, "You'll need it."

Wind Flower leaned back intending only to rest her eyes but, unexpected weariness overtook her. Before she knew it, she too was asleep—a deep, dangerous sleep full of dreams and remembrances. A sleep so deep that she failed to hear the horses. By the time the white man's voice broke into her dreams it was too late. Too late to run, too late to hide.

CHAPTER 2

Wind Flower found herself in a familiar dream. Lost in the woods, she spied Ni'hu, her father, through the trees, calling, beckoning for her. Running to him, she cried, begging him to hold her. As strong, gentle arms enfold her, Ni'hu whispers, "Be still, my daughter—you're safe." Suddenly, a shadowy figure steps into the clearing—a Washita, his blue eyes blazing into hers. "Come daughter," his eyes beseech her to follow. They are her own eyes gazing back at her. Ni'hu holds tight and she is safe, but the Washita stays too, close by, watching, waiting.

Suddenly Corn Woman's face replaces that of the Washita. Corn Woman, tall and proud with her long, black braids tinged with gray. It is Corn Woman and her troubles that have brought the people together for the Renewal of the Sacred Arrows. Her shame must be healed and her brother, Bear Claw, has pledged the arrow renewal to bring the tribe back into favor—his sister's disgrace had touched them all.

Corn Woman struck Small Willow, her daughter, and soon after, the young girl killed herself in shame. For this, Corn Woman had been banished from the tribe forever. But her leaving was not enough—bad luck hung over the tribe like a black cloud, smothering what little fortune remained.

The Cheyenne had had too much misfortune and now Bear Claw hoped to bring back the luck. The ceremony, coming as it did at the height of the hunting season, promised prosperity and hope for all. The Sweet Medicine Chief would guide the Cheyenne on their journey, his powerful wisdom and knowledge guiding them out of the darkness.

Once the ceremony began, all the women and children would be confined to the tipis for four days and night. Wind Flower recognized the importance of the arrow renewal, but she dreaded the confinement. Today the air had smelled especially sweet. In her dream, she breathed deeply, gulping up the sweet crisp air, hoping to hold on to a little, to take with her into the dark, stuffy tipi. As she breathed in, half-asleep, half-awake, the air suddenly changed, growing thicker and she began to choke.

"Hey, Cooky. What we got here? A couple of little squaws! Musta wandered off the reservation!" He'd already grabbed Laughing Dove. She screamed, struggling to free herself as the horses pawed the ground, circling them. Choking dust surrounded her as Wind Flower struggled to her feet. The man kept one arm around Laughing Dove's waist as he fought off the kicks and scratches of her older sister.

"Jesus, Cooky! Git off yer horse and help me. We got a regular wildcat here!"

Jumping from his horse, Cooky grabbed Wind Flower's arm pulling her away. "Well now little Missy. Ain't no call to carry on like that! We ain't gonna hurt ya. Gonna help, don't ya know? You'll be a dern sight better off where we's headed than you are now I reckon. Now settle down, you hear!" His breath reeked of tobacco and whiskey and his rough beard brushed against her cheek as he held her against him.

Laughing Dove called out, her wails echoing through the forest. Wind Flower kicked and scratched, desperately trying to free herself. "Ouch! Christ almighty, Les—the little hellcat bit me!" Raising his hand, he brought it down full force, knocking her to the ground.

Sometime later, Wind Flower woke to the jostling of the horse, a sharp, stabbing pain in the small of her back from the saddle horn pressed up against her. They rode in silence on a well-worn trail across open ground. The land was unfamiliar to Wind Flower. She attempted to sit up, but was pushed down roughly with a "Not so fast my little bobcat. After yer clawing, you kin suffer fer a bit."

Cranking her neck, she vainly tried to catch a glimpse of her sister, but the other man rode alongside Cooky, and she was unable to see over or around the horse. No sound came from the other riders, save the clopping of hooves on the hard, dusty ground of the trail. Closing her eyes, she beseeched the Wise Ones Above to help them.

It grew dark, the men began searching for a place to camp for the night. "We'll never make the train tonight, Cooky. Better to sleep here and make an early start."

At his words, Wind Flower woke with a start, her head fuzzy and sore. Cooky dragged her down, shoving her towards the others. Finally she spied her sister, discovering the reason for her silence. Laughing Dove had been gagged with Les' grimy bandanna, now soaked with her tears. Wind Flower tried to go to her, but Cooky yanked her back. "Oh no you don't. Get us some wood and hurry up."

When she pretended not to understand, he grabbed a fistful of twigs, gesturing, "Wood, you stupid squaw. Wood. And hurry up or your sister gets it," he added, pointing a hunting knife at Laughing Dove who cowered on the ground, eyes wild with fear. Wind Flower's eyes reached out to the frightened child, reassuring her in their gaze before she turned to hurry off for wood.

Wind Flower understood the men perfectly, but Laughing Dove knew not a word of English and with every word her fear escalated. Her older sister decided to feign ignorance as well, perhaps learning more of their plans if they thought she didn't understand their talk. Jack Wilkins, a scout who had lived with the tribe for a time had taught Wind Flower the white man's tongue. Jack, or Fire Hair, as the Cheyenne called the tall, gentle man with the head of flaming red hair, had lived for several moons in Lone Dove's tipi, but then he had been called away East. It had been twelve moons since they'd last seen him.

Jack said Wind Flower was a fast learner and urged her parents to enroll her in the government school. "She'd outshine them all," Jack told them, but Strong Arrow and Smooth Water wouldn't hear of it.

Hurrying to gather as many twigs and branches as she could, Wind Flower rushed back frantic with worry and longing to comfort her sister.

Where were they taking them? There had been so many stories circulating among her people. Tales of children abducted and sold into slavery in Mexico, but these men were not Mexicans—who were they? Her kindred always spoke of the white man and his devilish ways in hushed tones, breaking off the talk when children appeared. She felt so ignorant, so unprepared.

Dropping the twigs in front of the man called Les, she moved towards her sister. "Not yet," he snarled pulling her back. "Fire first, then the kid." He used the Cheyenne word for fire, then repeated it. "Fire."

Wind Flower was experienced in fire starting, a chore that had been hers alone for many moons and she soon had a small crackling fire blazing. The men brought food and cooking utensils from their saddle bags.

As they prepared dinner, she began inching her way towards Laughing Dove until she sat at her sister's side. She slid her arm around the trembling child and Laughing Dove collapsed against her sobbing. As the men appeared to take no notice of them, Wind Flower quietly slipped off the gag and the muffled sobs became audible.

Their captors turned and Cooky yelled, "Hey," but the other man said, "If she can shut up, it can stay off. If not, back on it goes. Understand?" He gestured with his hands and Wind Flower nodded, whispering to her sister, beseeching her to be silent. After several great sighs and heavings of breath, her weeping ceased, and she lay shivering in her sister's arms.

As he pulled a tin pot from the stove, Cooky motioned to them. "Come, eat." They were each given a bowl of something called hash that burned their throats and tasted horrible. The girls tried to eat, for fear of angering their captors, but the hash simply would not go down.

Finally, the men allowed them to retreat back from the fire to where their root bags lay forgotten on the ground. Wind Flower reached into hers for a turnip, intending to share it with Laughing Dove, but the cock of a pistol stopped her.

"Not so fast." Cooky's gun was aimed at her heart, his eyes, cold and empty, glaring down at her. Killer's eyes.

"Put it down, Cooky." Les pushed his partner's hand away, advancing towards the pair huddled on the ground. In their tongue he asked, "What's in the bag?"

In reply, Wind Flower spilled the contents onto her skirt. When he spied the small stash of roots and berries, Les laughed, "Yep Cooky, ya better shoot'em! That there's a dangerous bunch of loot they got theirselves." Cookie scowled, turning back towards the fire, ignoring Les who laughed until tears ran down his cheeks.

The girls chewed small pieces of turnip, comforted by the familiar tastes after the putrid hash. They huddled together on a blanket the men had thrown them until Les said, "Time to sleep little ones. Don't you be scared, now. We's taking you to school. Understand? School? Not gonna scalp you, or kill you. So you can rest easy."

His words made no sense to Wind Flower. What did he mean about school? Was he taking them back to the reservation school? If so, why had they grabbed them in the first place?

In spite of her fears, sleep soon overtook her, lulled by the even steady breathing of the child beside her. Laughing Dove had fallen asleep with the turnip still in her mouth. Fallen asleep, mid-chew.

Chapter 3

With the sun, they traveled many miles over rough, wild country, all of it strange to Wind Flower. Again, she rode with Cooky, sitting up this time instead of slung over the saddle like a dead animal. Cooky held the reins with one hand keeping the other firmly around her waist. Pressed as she was hard against the saddle horn, his hot, foul breath was inescapable. As they rode, he ran his hand up and down over her chest and his coarse lips brushed the back of her neck. For her sister's sake, Wind Flower put on a brave face, but shame and fear washed over her.

Willing her mind away, she thought of the rolling streams and cool woods of their camp. It had been wonderful to escape the confines of the reservation to ride out onto the prairie. Most of the year the soldiers kept them corralled into the small settlement area. This brief time—summer hunting season—was the only time her people were free to travel beyond the confines established by their white jailers. The Cheyenne no longer possessed land or the right to dwell on the earth they had roamed for centuries, restricted now to the barren acres along the Tongue River. This limited summer freedom had been allowed as long as Wind Flower could remember, but there were rumors and more Washita promises to be broken soon. She'd overheard the hushed voices at the evening campfires saying that this year might be the last when her people would be allowed to roam free, to hunt the buffalo that grew scarcer with each passing season.

Many more wagons had come. When the Washita needed more land; he would take it. That was the one certainty still left to her people—when the white man wanted something, he took it. If a treaty stood in his way, it would be broken. Nothing was sacred to the Washita, not his word, not his treaties, not even the earth which he stole, then laid to waste with his mining, his cattle, his iron horses and the senseless slaughter of the buffalo.

"Pretty little thing this," Cooky called. His right hand rested several times on her small breasts. "Maybe I'll just keep this one fer my squaw. Almost grown and—"

"Leave her be, fer the love of God, Cooky! We're almost to Round Tree and the train'll be waiting. She's still a kid. Get your hands down or we'll switch."

"From where I'm a sittin', she ain't no kid," he replied, but returned both hands to the reins. "Hey, Les, don't get yer fool back up. They're only redskins. Scum. Just a couple of wild animals, don't know any better. We could make a detour and—"

"Shut up and ride," Les had rested his gun. Cooky's hands were still for the rest of the ride and silently Wind Flower thanked the man called Les for his help.

Soon they came to a dusty, white man's town. People stared after the horses as the men made their way towards the train depot. Some children raced across in front of Cooky's horse, yelling, "Redskins, redskins—wish you were dead skins!"

"Outta the way kids," Les boomed.

As the children ran off the sounds of their taunts receding in the distance, Wind Flower wished she had never learned the white man's tongue. Her sister smiled watching the children, blissfully unaware of the cruelty of their words.

Les and Cooky dismounted, pulling their captives along as they scanned the crowds at the station. At length they spotted a tall, white man about Cooky's height neatly dressed in dark pants and a starched white shirt. He stood leaning against an open freight car, beckoning to them.

"Got two more fer ya, Happy," Cooky called, as they drew up.

"Okay, toss'em up with the rest. I'll pay ya next week when the payroll comes in."

"Nothin doin'," said Les. "We've come a long ways with these two. The older one's a real find and the little one just the sort they's lookin' fer up north. Pay us now or we'll take'em elsewhere. The slavers come through every week or so. They'll be right glad to get a hold of these two—believe me."

"Lester Carter. I'm speechless. What we're doin' here is the Lord's work. The Lord's and the U.S. government's. How can you ever think of selling these two to the Mexicans? Is that why you're in this, for the money? If you are you can just pack it in right now. Why, I—"

"Listen, Monroe. That's a loada horseshit and you know it. Give us the money, or the kids go on with us."

Reaching into his pocket, Happy drew out a small sack, handing it to Les. "Just testin' yer. Had it all counted out fer you boys, someone spotted ya headin' in."

He laughed, turning to Wind Flower. "And don't worry none darlin'. I would've never let 'em sell ya to those filthy Mexis. You're much too purty. You'll make a fine addition to them schools, what with you knowing English and all. Take care and behave. It's a might rough at first, but you'll make out fine."

Surprised, Wind Flower realized that she'd betrayed herself. She had been taught to cloak her face, never revealing thoughts and feelings to the Washita, but she had reacted to the man's words. The talk of slavers had brought fear to her eyes and the man called Happy had seen it.

They were thrust into a filthy cattle car. The stench hit them the second they stepped inside, robbing Wind Flower of breath like the first sighting of the buffalo herd each summer. Instead of the awe she felt after the first sighting of the buffalo she now found herself gagging, afraid to breathe lest she vomit. When she could hold her breath no longer, she gasped. The smell of sour dung, boards soaked with urine and rotten hay, dank with the smell of fear overwhelmed her. She wanted to cry out, to burst into tears, rush into a corner to hide, but knew she must be brave for her sister's sake.

As the nausea subsided and her eyes grew accustomed to the darkness, she scanned the room gasping again at her surroundings. All around them were children. There must have been 60 or 70, mostly younger than she. Some of them cried softly, a few wailed pitifully, but most lay silent and resigned. From the look of them, many had traveled a long way already. There were Arapaho, Blackfoot, Cheyenne, Sioux, and many others that she didn't recognize. Many were sick and delirious with fever; others lay listless with hunger and despair.

Finally, locating a spot to sit down, she cradled Laughing Dove in her arms, studying their fellow travelers more intently. Feeling for the few roots still left in her bag, she contemplated keeping them for later in case they needed them, but quickly decided to share them. Wind Flower was a good forager. If left on the prairie she knew she could keep her sister and herself alive.

"Come," she called softly in Cheyenne, showing them the tiny scraps of food. As the children moved listlessly towards her, the door of their prison slammed shut and the train began moving.

Cutting off tiny hunks of turnip—just enough to go around and give everyone something to chew on—she doled them out, keeping careful track so that everyone got a tiny share. Many of the children were too tired, sick or apathetic to rise and come forward, but the others brought them a piece.

As the train rumbled forth over the prairie, they sat silently chewing. Many were on the brink of starvation. Lately there had been little food on the reservation, but things had been worse for most of these children.

As the government supplies grew smaller and game grew scarcer with each passing season, her people continued to grow corn and other grains, but the land, hard and angry, gave back little. The woods still held promises. The precious days ceded by the Washita for foraging and hunting must not be wasted. Roots, plants and berries must be gathered and stored if the people were to make it through another winter.

Each spring was spent repairing and mending clothes and tattered tipis, almost beyond repair. The people needed the hides of buffalo, elk and deer to replace the worn, frayed hides of the tents.

The foods of spring would enable the people to live independently for a few months instead of waiting to receive the rotting grains and putrid meat doled out by the blue-coated soldiers. Chunks of dried meat and steaming bowls of soup, sweetened and flavored with turnips and the roots of the lily, were Wind Flower's favorite foods.

She shuddered thinking about the other seasons when the people were given food deemed unfit for Washita tables. For this, her people were expected to be grateful. And because they starved, the Cheyenne ate the food, growing weak and sickly. Confined to the barren land of the reservation they had little choice. She had often heard her parents say that the Cheyenne were better off than most; looking around the cattle car, she saw that they had been right.

The Renewal of the Sacred Arrows had held such promise of prosperity and hope. Now, for her mother and father, there would only be grief. Grief for the daughters stolen away. Lost, perhaps forever.

CHAPTER 4

As time passed Wind Flower grew accustomed to the noise of the train. She had long since swallowed her tiny piece of turnip, so she began to sing. One of Laughing Dove's favorites, it was the song of the doe and her fawns inching their way silently past the hunters to the safety of the mountains. As she sang, many of the little children crawled closer to them. Close enough to hold onto Wind Flower's skirt, shyly placing their heads on her legs and ankles. She felt warm and comforted by their touch and for a few minutes forgot her own fear of what lay at the end of the journey.

One tiny boy, a Dakota Sioux, crouched at her side through the night, whimpering softly. By his size, she guessed him to be about three. Despite the heat of the car, he shivered continually and his head burned with fever. She was afraid for Laughing Dove—afraid she might fall sick too—so she pushed her sister to the opposite side of her as far from the boy as possible. When Laughing Dove finally slept she took up the boy in her arms, cradling his shaking body. Murmuring softly, words of comfort and reassurance, she pressed her cool face against the cheeks burning with fire.

Always strong, seldom ill, Wind Flower had no fear for herself. White Deer, the tribal healer, often told her, "Some people are born strong like you, Flower. Favored by the Wise Ones to go through life as healers, tending for those less hardy in times of great sickness."

Laughing Dove on the other hand was frequently ill—always seemed to be complaining of something. Many times she would burn a fever, especially during the winter months. Washita food in particular seemed to sicken Laughing Dove but lately the tribe had more illness no matter what the season. The white man brought disease and sickness with him, in his food, his animals, in his belongings. Like a great cloud, the sicknesses hovered over the people, descending like heavy mists from which there was no escape. Creeping into tipis the white man's sickness was slowly poisoning the people, according to White Deer. As the train rumbled through the night, Wind Flower wondered if she would ever see White Deer again.

The Iron Horse stopped many times during the night. Several times Wind Flower awoke thinking they had reached their destination, only to feel the sickening lurch as they'd started moving again. Finally, not long after sunrise, she heard a piercing whistle and the train stopped for the last time. Voices surrounded the car. People yelled for help with bags, workers ran to unload the freight cars. A chorus of voices mingled with other sounds, merged into a steady, almost deafening hum, like the sound of locust swarming over the prairie fields.

Attempting to rise, she suddenly remembered her tiny charge still nestled in her lap. As he appeared to be sleeping she reached down, gently nudging him onto the hay beside them. As her hand touched his emaciated arm she drew back in recognition and fear. The arm was icy cold; his hand, rigid in death still grasped the hem of her skirt.

Tears rolled down her face as she whispered, "Child of the Dakotas. I will not forget you. Later, when we are safe, I will sing you a mourning song to help your journey into the spirit world." She realized, as she gazed down at his sleeping face, that she did not even know his name.

Gently working his fingers to free herself, she rose kneeling beside her sister. Laughing Dove's hair, damp with sweat, lay across her face just visible in the slats of sunlight peeking through the walls of the cattle car. When there is more light I will rebraid her hair, Wind Flower thought, gently pushing the soft locks from the child's face. Laughing Dove looks so peaceful in slumber, she thought sadly, knowing that in wakening peacefulness would give way to terror. "Wake up little one," she whispered, "We'll soon be out in the open air."

Laughing Dove's face scrunched up immediately and her sister braced herself for the temper tantrum that usually accompanied an abrupt awaking. Afterwards, she found herself almost wishing for a fit of temper instead of the shivering fear that she glimpsed in her sister's wakening eyes.

Accustomed now to the overwhelming stench in the car, Wind Flower none-theless longed to be up and out of the noxious prison. She watched the door, stroking Laughing Dove's hair to calm her as the others huddled around them for protection. The car had come alive with moving bodies, alert to the movements outside, watching and waiting.

At length the door swung open and a gruff voice called, "Everybody forward." As the group began to shuffle slowly towards the open door, Wind Flower led the way, holding her head up to give the others courage. In the daylight, she saw that she was the oldest by far. Most of the children looked to be Laughing Dove's age or younger. She must be brave.

"Come on, ye little heathens," yelled the same voice, no less friendly now. "We ain't got all day. People's awaitin' for all ye little savages, though I can't imagine why. A filthy lot you are too! Jesus, Mary and Joseph, what a stench!" He pulled them out, roughly shoving the frightened group to the side until all but four remained in the car. Three sickly ones and the tiny Sioux. Wind Flower tried to hop up and help a girl who lay moaning softly to the right of the door, but the man shoved her back snarling, "Over there you. I'll take care of the shirkers. Hey, Bill," he called over his shoulders. "We got a couple of sick ones here and looks like a dead one in back, too. Bring a couple of crates to cart 'em in and make it quick. Padre's anxious to get back to morning mass and Woody's itching to leave fer the Academy."

The man called Bill brought a long empty box into which two of the sickly children were thrown. Both girls were unconscious now and seemed unaware of the rough treatment they were receiving. A second box was produced for a slightly older boy. As he was larger in size, his box proved more unwieldy once loaded and Bill called for help with it. At first the boy screamed, but after the box slipped and fell, several times crashing to the station floor, he cried out no more.

The burly man, with hair on his face and little on his head, began herding them into the main part of the station. Between the benches, the bedraggled band stumbled along past the ticket windows and out through the entrance. No one seemed to take any notice of them until they stepped into the sunlight again. At once several men advanced towards the children, waving their hands and gesturing to the man.

"It's high time, Potter. I've been here since before dawn waiting. Is this the lot of them?" A short man approached them, his face set in an angry grimace. He was dressed in a long, black robe and funny black hat, perched like a mushroom on top of his head. Around his neck a long chain swung back and forth as he moved. At the end of the chain hung the white man's cross, gold and glimmering in the morning sunlight. The man in black frightened Wind Flower and she shrank back, pulling Laughing Dove with her.

"Beg pardon Padre, but we's been promised half this shipment. Miss Wilson's got her heart set on it. 'Specially as this is a young bunch. She 'specially asked for young ones." This man resembled Les somewhat, with the same long legs and scraggly hair sticking out of his hat. Squinting in the bright light, he shielded his eyes with a rough, red hand, surveying them critically. Wind Flower thought that he winked at the bald man, but couldn't be sure.

"Mr. Woodson, of course I am prepared to share with the good Miss Wilson, but as the Lord's work always comes before all others, I, of course, will have the first pick. There's plenty here for everyone." The man in black smiled, a crooked, unfriendly smile, his eyes like the wolf's before he springs for the kill. Wind Flower pressed Laughing Dove behind her, shrinking farther back, praying to the Great Spirits that the man in black would not choose them.

"Well now, Padre. Miss Wilson told me you'd say something like that and I'm powerful sorry, but I'm obliged to contradict the Lord in this instance. Miss Wilson—she specifically said we was to take turns picking till they was all gone. Said it was the only fair way t'a do it and that I was not t'a let you buffalo an old softy like myself."

The man in black opened his mouth to protest, but was interrupted by the hairy faced man who said, "He's right, Padre. Let's get on with it. I'm fillin' two orders here and you and the Lord don't have no priority. Git busy and choose up the little heathens and let's move along. We got decent folks waiting fer trains here and they don't need the stench of this bunch puttin' 'em off their breakfasts."

"You begin, Father. I'll go second," the man called Woodson generously offered. The man in black recognizing defeat, pointed to an Arapaho girl, not more than three, and the choosing commenced. As they were near the back of the group, the sisters were not noticed right away. Wind Flower crouched when the Padre chose and stood tall when it was the man called Woodson's turn to choose.

Only a few children remained when she heard Woodson call, "I'll take the tall one. Load her on with the others." Wind Flower was shoved towards the cowering group of Mr. Woodson's "picks."

"Wait a minute, Woodson," it was the man in black and he had spotted Laughing Dove, hiding behind her sister, clutching her skirt. "Trying to get two for the price of one? Pull the little one out and keep her."

Laughing Dove was torn away, her arms pinned back as she was held up for the Padre's approval. "I'll take her," he called harshly. "Finally, a healthy one after all these others." Wind Flower screamed, running to her sister, throwing her arms around her, refusing to let go.

"Get that dirty savage off my student and load the little one in," called the Padre. "I've seen enough."

They tried to pry her hands apart, striking her several times in the struggle, but Wind Flower would not let go. She scratched, Laughing Dove screamed, and the men yelled. The other children witnessing the sisters' plight began to wail and soon the whole group was crying and howling. The hairy-faced man did most of the hitting; the man called Woodson stood watching nearby. Just as they'd succeeded in prying them apart, Mr. Woodson called, "Say, Padre, this looks like a dark one. Won't look none too good in yer starchy white uniforms neither. Let me take the both of 'em off your hands and I'll cart away the sick ones too. There's three of 'em and they're pretty bad off. Be a good deal fer you. What 'dya say?"

"Very well, Woodson," said the padre, hopping into his wagon. "Take her—she looks like trouble anyway—but next time I will choose first again. Remember that." Woodson tipped his hat as the hairy-faced man loaded the last of the Padre's children into the wagon and they rolled away from the station. Wind Flower's heart flew out to the little ones so frightened and small huddled in the back of the wagon. She wished they could have all come with Laughing Dove and herself with the man called Woodson instead to the house of the man in black.

Woodson, with the other man's help, loaded them into another wagon and they too were on their way. The children huddled together as the cart rumbled out of town into the countryside bouncing them over the rutted, bumpy road. They all held hands and Wind Flower tried to sing a little over the din. She sang of the fox, wily and cunning, as he leaps through the tall grass looking for food. Thinking of the little fox bounding along gave the children courage. Courage enough to smile a little—at least those who understood the words. The others seemed reassured by the smiles around them and rhythm of her song even if the words were lost.

At last they stopped and Mr. Woodson called, "All out! Here we are, Mis Wilson!"

Dust swirled around the wagon for several minutes, clouding her vision. Wind Flower covered her eyes and waited for it to settle. After a time, she dared to open them and peering up, she had her first glimpse of Rose Academy.

The red brick walls seemed to rise up to the top of the sky. Twin towers at either end thrust out, daring all comers to challenge their authority. In the center of the building close to the ground a huge wooden door stood open to the morning breezes. Framed in the massive wood entryway, her hands folded in front of her, stood the tallest white woman Wind Flower had ever seen.

She'd seen many white men over the years, but their women seldom ventured onto the reservation. With the exception of a few settlers encountered in their travels, she knew little of the white woman. Perhaps this fact made her initial impression of Miss Wilson all the more striking. The woman had a stern, hard face, but her eyes seemed softer, at least for an instant. In that first glance, they reminded Wind Flower of her na'go, her mother's youngest sister's deep set eyes—dark and gentle.

When the woman spoke, the spell was broken and her eyes clouded over, changing from soft, rippling pools to black ice. "Mr. Woodson, bring them around. Nurse and Christina are waiting for them in the wash room."

"What 'bout the sick ones, marm? They cain't hardly stand up, p'rhaps washin' ain't best fer them just yet."

Miss Wilson strode out, peering into the boxes that held the three children. "Good God, Woodson. What's happened here?" She pulled one of the boxes out, the one that held the boy. "Who's responsible for this?" Wind Flower peeked over the edge of the box and could tell by the

odd angle at which the body rested that the boy was dead. Dried blood on his forehead suggested that rough treatment, rather than fever, had been the cause of his demise.

"Where did this child come from and how did he end up like this?" Not waiting for Mr. Woodson's reply, she continued, "Oh Lord, for goodness sakes, get the others in. Don't let's have them gawking!"

"Twern't my fault, marm," Woodson protested as he herded the terrified band around to the back of the building. "T'was that feller over ta the station. Ain't got no feelins er nothin'."

His words were lost on Miss Wilson. As they rounded the corner out of view, Wind Flower saw the tall woman lift the other box containing the two girls, carrying it towards the open door. She noticed that the woman wielded the load easily and did not appear in need of assistance.

"Come on, kids. Let's get this over with. Worst part of the trip really, then you'll be all fixed up." He swung open a door leading them down a narrow passageway, the clacking of his heavy boots echoing in the empty hallway. Finally, the shuffling band reached an open doorway. "Okay, all of you in here. The ladies'll be along to see to you shortly."

CHAPTER 5

The room was bare, except for long, wooden benches running around the perimeter. Directing them all to "sit and stay put," the man named Woodson left, closing the door behind him. At his departure Wind Flower rose, wondering if this might be their first opportunity to escape. Pulling Laughing Dove along beside her, she had barely reached the door when she heard voices approaching. "How many have we got today, Woodson?"

"Near to thirty I'd expect, Miss C. Want me to take a head count?"

"Never mind. Nurse and I'll take care of it. You run along and stay out in back in case any of them try to—"

"Don't you fret none marm. I'll be out back if you need me."

Wind Flower pulled her sister to the far end of the room and sat down just as the door swung open and a short, stocky woman with red cheeks, brown frizzy hair and dark eyes burst in. "Nurse," she called over her shoulder. Scanning the room, she was silent for a short time during which a taller woman, dressed all in white, came up and tapped her on the shoulder.

"I'm ready, Christina. What have we today?"

"Looks like twenty-six of the filthy heathens, Margaret. Lord, what a stench! Better put extra kerosene in the buckets today, they'll be full of lice! Eight boys, the rest girls. Poor Harriet took two sick ones in to bathe herself. You really should be up with her, but I can't manage the lot myself and you don't see the teachers volunteering. Too far hoighty-toighty for this type of work, aren't they? Filthy savages! Better off dead if you ask me."

"Now, Christina. With your dear father's support, Harriet does tremendous work here. Taking these young ones away from their hopeless lives and giving them opportunities. Rescuing them from the darkness of their savage past." The taller woman, called Margaret or Nurse, had stepped into the room and was peering around critically at them. Her face was as white as her dress. The skin stretched tight as a bow string, blended into one continuous line with her straw-colored hair that was wound into a tight knot at the base of her neck. Despite her extreme appearance, her eyes were soft, hazel buttons possessing none of the cruelty that blazed like a prairie fire in the eyes of her companion.

"Still—better off dead, I say. Come Margaret, let's get on with it."

They each grabbed a child. The first to go were a brother and sister who clung to each other on a bench near the door. They were Pawnee, very small and thin. They whimpered as the women ripped them apart and dragged them from the room. Soon they heard cries and screams from the far end of the hallway, then silence. Not long after, a door clanged and footsteps approached. The women were back for two more victims.

Finally, their turn came. The sisters went out together, fighting and clinging to one another. Halfway down the hall the two women finally succeeded in separating them. Miss Christina latched hold of Wind Flower with an iron grasp. As Laughing Dove continued to cry and scream, Wind Flower called, "I am here sister, don't worry! I am here with you!"

Reaching the end of the hallway, they were thrust into a dark room. The door was slammed and locked behind them. The large and cold room had a stone floor sloping downward towards the middle. There appeared to be a hole in the center covered by a metal circle and Wind Flower tried to approach the hole to peer into it.

"Oh, no you don't," Miss Christina snarled, as she propelled her forward, hurling her to the floor in front of a wooden bucket filled with brown water.

Glancing over, Wind Flower spied Laughing Dove in the same position on the opposite end of the room.

It was but a second's glance. Before she knew what was happening, her dress was torn from her body, ripped to shreds, and tossed aside. "Everything off," Miss Christina hissed as Wind

Flower clung to tattered hides still ringing her waist. With sharp, stabbing fingers, the woman wrested the remaining shreds from her captive, heaving them into a pile in the corner.

"The fire's too good for that filth, you little beast. And what have we here?" she mocked, holding her captive's wrists, gazing down at Wind Flower's budding breasts. "Quite the little woman, aren't we? Disgusting— would you look at this Margaret! Lord, I hate it when they send these older ones. Probably too late to redeem this one, but at least she's not as black as that little filth you're wrestling with. Let's hope it'll clean up better than it looks!"

With that she pushed Wind Flower down, holding her neck so tightly that breath refused to come. "Better hold your nose and close your mouth or get ready for a mouthful of kerosene. Lord, what am I talking to you for? Dumb thing can't understand me anyway!"

Just as the fire water reached her face Wind Flower heard her sister cry out. It was a scream she would never forget—full of terror and surprise. Then she too cried out, forgetting to close her mouth, her eyes instantly blinded by the fire pouring over her head. When her hair was soaked, it was thrust into the barrel of brown water and other stinging water replaced the first. Her body was then scrubbed with a hard, scratching brush that cut into her skin, causing the brown water to sting even more.

Fearing more fire and pain, Wind Flower kept her eyes clamped shut as she was led, blindly stumbling, to another corner of the room. When she dared open her eyes a crack, she found her vision blurred. She could distinguish forms and shapes, but little else. Her eyes burned with pain.

As she struggled to see more clearly, Miss Christina shoved her down upon a wooden crate. The floor all around was wet, but soft, different than the stone floor they had been forced to kneel upon. Squinting down, Wind Flower tried to discern what accounted for the softness beneath her feet. Unable to see clearly, she reached down and grabbed a clump of wet brown softness, bringing it close to her face.

Even with blurred vision she recognized it—hair. Immediately she struggled, trying to free herself, but Miss Christina slapped her down, "Stay put, you ignorant heathen, or I'll shave your head too!" Grabbing her long braid, the woman twisted it round her hand. There was no escape. In the time it took Wind Flower to draw a breath, her beautiful hair, never shorn since the day she was born, lay on the floor with that of the other children.

Yanking her along by what scant hair remained, Miss Christina threw Wind Flower into a smaller, adjoining room where Laughing Dove had already been taken. Opening her eyes, she found that they still stung with searing pain, but her vision had cleared and she could see her sister. The other woman, Margaret, struggled to dress the child in a loose-fitting blue garment. Her hair, too, had been shorn, the beautiful black braids left behind on the stone floor. What hair she still possessed, stuck out at odd angles all over her head, stiff and hard from the stinging waters.

Laughing Dove cried when she spied her sister. They vainly struggled to reach one another but iron hands held them back. Wind Flower was also fitted with a blue dress, given undergarments that fit like men's trousers and trailed down below her knees. Made of coarse white fabric, they chafed her legs when she walked.

Over the blue dresses went white squares of cloth the women called pinafores. The pinafores tied in the back, making Wind Flower feel trapped in her clothes— like a wolf in a pitfall covered with earth and grass.

"Come on then," said the big woman called Christina. "Time for the next two. I'll take them up, Margaret. Better get Woody to get you some fresh water. That batch is vile. Waste of good water, but it can't be helped."

Pulling the sisters along the corridor, she shoved them up a flight of stairs, carefully keeping them apart, one on each arm.

When they reached the landing they stood on a wooden floor, much softer on their bare feet than the stone floor below. She dragged them down another hallway, stopping at length and shoving them to sit on a long bench. "Stay put," she growled, disappearing through an open doorway.

Shortly afterward she returned with the tall woman they had seen upon their arrival. Miss Christina bustled away without a word and Wind Flower was not sorry to see her go.

"Hello. I know you cannot understand me," spoke the stern voice. "But, you will. Soon you will be speaking right along with all of the other students. We will take care of you from now on. This is your home. You must forget everything about your past. It is dead. You have no families, but those of us here at Rose Academy. We are your family and will provide for all your needs. You may speak only English, you may think only English and you will be punished if you disobey. I don't like to punish, but it's for the best. In the end you will thank me for it. Now, Miss Craven." She called over her shoulder and another woman appeared. "Miss Craven, what names have we for these two new girls?"

"We're up to Rachel and Ruth on the list, Miss Wilson."

"Very well. You," she pointed to Laughing Dove, "You will be Rachel. And you," she said to Wind Flower, "You, my dear, shall be Ruth. Rachel - Ruth, Rachel - Ruth."

As she repeated the names she poked their chests. A sweet smell of bottled flowers seemed to surround her and Wind Flower tried not to gag. "Can you say Rachel?" she pointed to Laughing Dove. Laughing Dove immediately began prattling in the Cheyenne tongue, uncertain of what was expected of her. "Miss Craven. The strap. It is time for our first lesson," the tall woman said briskly.

A strip of leather was produced and before the sisters knew what was happening, Laughing Dove's hand received three lashes in quick succession. When Wind

Flower tried to intervene, the strap licked her face, raising an angry welt. Startled, she fell back onto the floor. When she rose Miss Craven leapt over to hold her, while the tall woman spoke to Laughing Dove. "No," she said, pointing to the child's lips and shaking her head. "Only English."

Laughing Dove whimpered, big tears rolling down her face, as she gazed at the woman called Wilson with surprise and fear in her eyes. "That's enough for now, Miss Craven. Take them up and show them their places in the dormitory. They'll need shoes too, of course. It's almost lunch time, so hurry along."

With those words they were led away up more stairs to a long, narrow room filled with what Wind Flower recognized as Washita beds. She had seen beds such as these once when the people had come upon an abandoned settler's cabin. Strange, sleeping mats on legs, they looked like they might run away with their occupants as they slept. Every bed was the same, covered with a white cloth at the head and a brown, scratchy blanket at the foot. She was led to one and Miss Craven pointed, "Ruth, this is your bed. Bed. Don't worry, your sister won't be far away. Come and see."

She led them into another smaller room with more beds and at length stopped and said, "Rachel, this is your bed. Bed." Laughing Dove gazed up at her and looked as if she might speak again, but bit her lip, staying silent. She learns fast, her sister thought sadly.

After fitting them with leggings—scratchy tubes of cloth that stretched over their legs—the girls were given white socks and hard-soled shoes that pinched their feet, causing Laughing Dove to cry again when she attempted to walk in them. "There, there little one," said Miss Craven. "You'll break them in no time and then they'll be nice and comfortable. A little stiff at first, that's all!"

She then led them to a room downstairs where the other new children now sat, leaving them alone. "Lunch will be soon. I'll be back to escort you in a few minutes." Her words were greeted blankly by all in the room including Wind Flower who had decided to feign ignorance as well.

Laughing Dove crawled into her lap and she whispered softly to her sister, telling her all the rules she hadn't understood. Wind Flower wished that she had the courage to call out to all the

children, saving them from the lash with her warnings, but she was frightened and the thought of the strap and the fire water made her hold her tongue. She had had enough for one morning.

CHAPTER 6

Lunch—the white man's meal, eaten when the sun is highest. It seemed to Wind Flower a strange time to eat and it would take a long time for the children to grow accustomed to the school meals. Rough, wooden bowls dripping with thin, watery oats, foul-smelling stew and always the tall glasses of milk made their stomachs cry out in pain.

As newcomers, the children were herded into the dining hall together. The teachers and Miss Christina endeavored to arrange them in a straight line, but it proved a futile task. They had work enough getting everyone seated. Lines would come later.

The sisters tried to stay together, but were quickly parted. "Younger girls to the right, older ones to the left." When Wind Flower ventured too far to the left, she was yanked back by Miss Christina. "Where do you think you're going, you little harlot? You'd like to sit with the boys, wouldn't you?"

Looking up she spied a table of older boys ahead and bowed her head, embarrassed and ashamed. As she followed the fat dorm mistress, Miss Christina asked to no one in particular, "What's the little harlot's name anyway?"

"Miss Christina. I remind you that this is a school," Miss Wilson spoke softly, but her voice reminded Wind Flower of the cragged cliffs at lost Chokeberry Creek. Hard and unyielding. "We do not use such language around the children. Is that clear?"

"Little wretch can't understand a word I say."

"That is hardly the point now, is it? Enough, please. Let's take our places." Her tone did not invite further conversation. The two women seated themselves at the teachers' table and Wind Flower found her place.

On a raised platform at the far end of the room, the teachers' table gave a clear vantage point from which jailers could view inmates, however, after seating themselves, the teachers did not appear to pay the students the slightest heed.

Bowls of a pasty mess resembling the hash Cooky and Les had served on the trail were plunked down in front of them. Wind Flower's stomach turned over at the sight of it, but she swallowed hard and prepared to eat. As she reached her hand toward the dish, the girl next to her caught it, shaking her head, "No, no, not yet."

Suddenly everyone except the new arrivals had their heads bowed. After a short period of silence, they sang briefly, something about God, the Great Spirit of the Washita, and how thankful they were for the food. Wind Flower liked the song and wondered if they would sing it again so that she might learn the words.

"You may begin girls." The august voice of Miss Wilson echoed down the length of the dining room and everyone began eating.

Once again, she reached her hand into the bowl. This time it was slapped away from behind. A tall older girl stood behind her frowning. "No, no. The spoon." She pointed to a metal spoon beside Wind Flower's bowl, then to the girls sitting around her. "Spoon," the monitor repeated. "You must eat with your spoon."

Wind Flower watched carefully for a short time and then tried it. Much smaller than the wooden spoons she was used to, the cold, metal implement gave her a bit of trouble at first with its delicate size and funny grip. However, after a few moments of practice, she managed to scoop the food up and get it into her mouth with only a little spillage. So preoccupied was she in the learning of how to use her spoon that she almost forgot about the horrible tasting hash.

Her bowl was nearly empty when she felt her stomach turning over. Swallowing hard again and again, she endeavored to force the food back down her throat, but to no avail. Up it came, back into the bowl before she could even rise out of her chair. Too dizzy and confused to even be embarrassed, she looked up spying the shocked faces all around her. As the only new girl at her table, she had received stares and curious glances all through lunch. Now they really had something to stare at.

"We've got a mess here, Miss Wilson."

"Make her eat it again," yelled Miss Christina. "It's one thing for the little ones, but she's old enough to know better! What a nuisance!"

"Leave her be, Christina. Annabelle, please take Ruth to the washroom so she can clean up. Then I'd like to see her in my office, please."

A young woman with yellow hair and kind eyes came forward, leading Wind Flower from the room. She could see several of the younger newcomers being led out by other teachers, also victims of the hash. She noticed that Laughing Dove was not among them and she tried to break free, to go to her, but the woman with the yellow hair held her tightly, whispering, "Not now, dear. You come along with me. You can see your little friends later."

She took her to a room adjoining the sleeping room. It was a long, narrow space with buckets of water set out in a neat row on a long, white shelf that ran the length of the room. Unlike Miss Christina's foul smelling water, the water in these buckets was clean and fresh. There were hard blocks of soap beside the buckets and white cloths hanging on hooks beneath the shelves.

Miss Annabelle wet the end of a cloth and said, "Here, let's see now. This cool towel will make your face feel much better and I expect you'll be needing a toothbrush. Have you been given one yet?" When Wind Flower stared blankly at her, she went to a cupboard in the corner and produced a tiny brush.

"There now. I'll show you." After dipping the brush in water she guided Wind Flower's hand to her mouth, brushing her teeth up and down. Because she was gentle, Wind Flower did not protest. The brush tickled her mouth till she started to giggle. "There's a smile from you," the woman smiled. "Why you're a lovely girl when you smile. I wish you were to be my student, but I have the younger ones. Perhaps I'll teach your little sister. I saw you two together. She is your sister, isn't she?"

Without thinking, Wind Flower nodded and in that one second gave away the secret she had guarded so closely. "You do understand English, don't you? I thought so. I'm so glad. You're a big strong girl and will be a wonderful example to the others. Can you speak as well?"

Nodding, Wind Flower still refused to speak. "Well, there's no hurry. Once you've settled in you'll have plenty to talk about."

She led Wind Flower to Miss Wilson's office where they found the headmistress sitting behind a wooden desk. It was a massive piece with many drawers and piles of papers and books covering its surface. To one side sat a green, glass ball. Trapped inside the glass were many tiny bubbles. Wind Flower wanted to grab the ball and shake it, to see if the bubbles might move about or fall out but, remembering the strap, she kept her hands at her side.

"Well now. You're looking much better, my dear. Come sit down." She began to gesture and mime, but Miss Annabelle said, "That's not necessary, Miss Wilson. Ruth understands English, quite well, I believe."

"I see. Well, thank you, Miss Annabelle, that will be all for now. Ruth and I will have a nice chat and Miss Grayson will see to her afterward. Better run up and check on your students. Rachel, Ruth's sister will be anxious to make your acquaintance I'm sure."

"Thank you, Miss Wilson. I'll see you later on Ruth," she said, patting her shoulder and winking as she departed. Until she gave away her secret, Wind Flower had rather liked Miss Annabelle, but suddenly the woman's tone and mocking words made her feel ashamed and angry. She decided that she didn't trust the smiling Miss Annabelle anymore than she did Miss Christina.

"Now then, Ruth. What can you tell me about yourself?" Wind Flower sat silent, not ready to speak. Her eyes still stung from the fire water and her stomach churned and rolled with the remnants of the hash.

"Come, come child, speak up. This silly game has gone on long enough. This is your home now. You have no need of your old ways or your language. Best to practice your English so you can get on in your new life."

"My name is Wind Flower and I want to go home." Her voice, unusually loud and gruff, reverberated in the quiet room.

"This is quite impossible. The area from which you were taken has been thoroughly cleaned out by the soldiers. We just heard today. Your people are most likely gone, scattered to who knows where.

"I'm sorry, but that's the truth my dear. You have no home to go back to, I'm afraid. Your tribe is no longer welcome on your old reservation. The land was needed by the settlers and the government has repossessed it. So you see how much better off you are here.

"Oh for pity sakes, stop your sniveling. I am sympathetic to your feelings, but Miss Christina will not be, I can assure you. She already seems to have taken a disliking to you and that makes for a rocky start. I'll endeavor to help you when I can but you must try, my dear. Do you understand what I'm telling you, Ruth?"

"My name is Wind Flower and I want to go home." She didn't believe a word the woman spoke. Miss Wilson's eyes shifted when she spoke, as people do when they are telling an untruth.

Flinching ever so slightly at Wind Flower's defiance, she went on, her voice controlled and even, "My dear child, that reply will become very tiresome, especially if Miss Christina hears you. I expect you to set a good example for the other girls. For an Indian, you are quite handsome, and your light skin and blue eyes will be great assets. Don't squander them with belligerence. I asked you here for this little talk because of your extraordinary features. Mark my words, they will carry you far if you let them! Why, with training and help, you could almost pass for a white girl. You are very lucky, Ruth. I hope you understand what I'm telling you.

"Let me explain a little of what's in store for you as you settle in. Miss Christina is the dorm mistress for the older girls. That means she will supervise your bedtime and rising and see that you are properly dressed, that your manners are correct and that you keep yourself and your possessions tidy. I tell you this because she may not be terribly helpful at first, hoping to trip you up these first few days.

"I would like you to succeed, Ruth, I really would. So many of the children here are dark and wild. In you I see a shining star. With your light eyes and fair complexion you might eventually be fully assimilated into decent English society. That is a worthy goal to strive for and one to which few of our students can aspire. Yes, my dear, if you study hard and mind your manners, there's a bright future ahead for you! Be respectful of Miss Christina and she will soften a little as time goes on.

"She is the daughter of our founder, Nathaniel Rose, and as such holds a position of some stature. She runs our boarding facility with a firm, efficient hand. She's strict and a bit rough in her methods, but you'll get used to her. Her father, old Mr. Rose, lives in town. Although he's retired, he occasionally pays us a visit.

"Your teachers will be Mr. Morgan and Miss Pyle. He teaches mathematics, geography and science and Miss Pyle will instruct you in literature and home economics, sewing, cooking and so forth. Have you any questions?"

"My name is Wind Flower and I want to go home."

"Oh my, that is tedious. Well, no matter—you'll learn, but I suspect it will be the hard way. Come, I'll take you to your classroom now."

Miss Wilson led the way out of her office down another hallway to the rear of the building. They proceeded through a pair of heavy, wooden swinging doors into another corridor, then a second set of doors bringing them into another building.

"This is our classroom building, my dear. You will spend every morning and every afternoon here with your lessons. Then, at four, you will return to your dormitory for a short rest period. After resting, you will come to me for manners instruction.

"After manners class, you'll have dinner, then study hall, then right to bed. It's a busy schedule. Our hope is that you will quickly forget your dark origins, looking forward instead to the bright future for which we are preparing you. Believe me, my dear, the sooner you leave your past behind the better. It's for the best—you'll see. You have no idea of the opportunities that await you in this new life. You are a very fortunate girl, Ruth."

Following the tall woman through the passageways of Rose Academy, Wind Flower thought of the other's words, "Your light skin and blue eyes will be assets." After a lifetime of ridicule with her people, enduring the taunts of her darker-skinned peers, her blue eyes and light complexion were now considered "assets."

Those who did not know her history, often remarked at how different the sisters were—seven years apart in age and worlds apart in appearance. Always slender and tall for her age, Wind Flower's eyes were the color of the wild cornflower that had given her her name. Not Ni'hu's eyes, but the eyes of the Washita father she had never known—the Washita who had raped Smooth Water during a raid on the people's camp. The Washita who had ridden away, leaving her young, beautiful mother beaten and half-dead.

No more than a girl, Smooth Water had wanted to die, begged to be left alone after the attack, refusing to eat or take shelter. Her sisters and White Deer had nursed her back to health. Refusing to give up, they had reached out and pulled her back from the spirit world.

Ni'hu, her father, was much older than Smooth Water. He had been thirty-two at the time of the raid and had lost his mate, Rushing Brook, two winters past. Ni'hu or Strong Arrow as he was known, had been a great hunter, but age and illness had weakened him and he was no longer able to ride with the hunters. Instead he became a toolmaker, fashioning the knife blades, fish hooks, spear points and many other tools necessary for tribal existence.

Strong Arrow courted Smooth Water slowly, realizing her ordeal had left her with many scars. When she finally consented to share his fire, he had won her over with kindness and love. Although they brought six children into the world, only Laughing Dove remained. Laughing Dove and his adopted daughter, Wind Flower. Wind Flower, "the flower of my heart" he called her and had raised her as his own.

The sisters grew up loved and nurtured. The family's hopes rested on their marriages. Their husbands would provide for Ni'hu and Na'go in their old age. Would provide the hides and meat that Strong Arrow could no longer bring home himself.

Wind Flower's bleeding had begun with the last moon. As she developed into womanhood, her breasts budded and her body grew round, soft curves replacing the thin boyish figure of her childhood. Already her na'gos, her mothers, had begun to acquaint her with the mysteries that lay ahead. Already they talked of marriage for her—marriage during the next hunting season.

Both sisters' marriages were necessary to ensure that Smooth Water and Strong Arrow would live a dignified, comfortable old age. What would they do now, Wind Flower thought, stifling a tear. What would her parents do without help and the comfort of their children?

CHAPTER 7

"Ah, here we are," Miss Wilson announced, knocking on the closed door in front of them. "This is Miss Pyle's room."

Almost immediately the door was opened by a slender woman slightly taller than Wind Flower. She stepped into the hallway, closing the door behind her.

"Miss Pyle, this is Ruth. Ruth, may I present your teacher, Miss Pyle. It is proper to shake hands, my dear. Like this," she said, demonstrating by shaking the other woman's hand. "Now you try it."

"Hello, Ruth," Miss Pyle smiled, taking the reluctantly proffered hand in her own. "Welcome to Rose Academy and to our class. The others will be so glad to meet you. Thank you, Miss Wilson, shall I take her from here?"

"Thank you, Emma," the other said, turning to go. "And don't take any nonsense from this one. Belligerent little thing, but she'll learn and don't spare the strap on her! Oh ... and she understands English quite well, despite her efforts to conceal it so whatever you do, do not coddle her! There's great potential in this Ruth of ours, but a strong will too!"

Turning to Wind Flower, Miss Wilson added, "Good luck my dear. I'll see you later on today, after rest time, for your first manners class. And do try and give us a chance, Ruth. Please." With those words, the headmistress turned on her heel and disappeared down the hallway.

"Come in then," the teacher said, putting her arm around her shoulders. Wind Flower was suddenly faced with row upon row of curious faces, all directed at her.

"Class, this is Ruth, one of our newest arrivals. Can you say hello?"

A singsong chorus of "Hello, Ruth" greeted her as she was directed to a seat near the back of the room.

"You are so nice and tall Ruth and you already know English so I'm sure the back will be fine for you. I shall depend on your help!"

She handed Wind Flower a blackboard that she called a "slate," and a piece of something called "chalk." She also gave her a small book. "This is your reader. You may take it to the dormitory with you this evening and practice during study hall. I've already given everyone tonight's assignment, but I'll show you at the end of class. Now then class, we are on page 24. Here you are," she said, handing her the book and pointing to some marks on the open page. "You may follow along as the others read. Robert, please resume where you left off."

A tall boy, several desks in front of her, began talking while looking at his book. Miss Pyle sat beside her, running her slender finger along the marks as he told the story. Wind Flower watched the finger, Miss Pyle's pink nails, perfectly rounded crescents, like the tiny, seashells brought west with the people who lived near the wide water. She watched, but had no idea why Miss Pyle sat running her finger over the paper.

The reading continued with several other children taking turns telling the story. She was amazed at the stories they seemed to make up as they went along, amazed that the next could take up where the other had left off, telling the tales in the same voice and tempo. They must have practiced many times, she thought listening as Miss Pyle's pink fingernails continued to slide back and forth over the pages.

The first story had been about a boy tending sheep. He cried "wolf" many times, bringing his worried people out to the fields to help him, only to discover they had been tricked. She thought about Ni'hu and the whipping she would have received had she lied like the sheep boy while tending the ponies. The boy in the story, whose name was Johann, had been sorry in the end. When he cried wolf on the fifth day, he cried in earnest as a hungry wolf crept closer to the flock. This time no one ran to help because no one believed him. Many sheep were killed by the wolf, including a beautiful lamb that belonged to Johann.

The lamb reminded Wind Flower of her foal, Water Eyes, born with the last moon. She had always known that she would not be allowed to keep her—ponies were much too valuable to the hunters—but she had nursed her and watched over her until the pony's wobbly legs had straightened and she was strong. Ni'hu said that she had been born too early and her mother was not yet ready for her. Every day Wind Flower had made a mash of goat's milk and grains to feed the wobbly-kneed colt. Not as nourishing as her mother's milk, but it had kept her alive. Wondering sadly if she would ever see Water Eyes again, Wind Flower's eyes misted over and she bit down on her lip to hold back the tears.

The next story was like a song, the words dancing merrily as the children told it. It was the tale of a bird whose feathers were dull and brown, but whose song brought joy and beauty to all that heard it. When the reader, a girl named Sarah, had finished, Miss Pyle asked, "Class, does anyone know what bird this is about?"

When no one volunteered an answer, she said, "Well, the poem does not say, but I believe it is the nightingale the poet writes about. After the next selection, I will read you the story of the 'Nightingale' by Hans Christian Anderson. Amy, you may start the next story, entitled, 'Harry and Annie."

The last story proved the least interesting. It told of two silly children walking out on the ice and falling in. They seemed very stupid to Wind Flower and she couldn't help thinking that "Harry and Annie'" was more like a lesson than a story. Her classmates seemed to know it well and she listened as they told it with one voice and cadence. There was a picture in her book of a girl she assumed must be Annie falling on the ice in a mound of fur and cloth. She wondered, studying the picture, how Annie could even walk, much less waddle out onto the ice, with all those ruffles and piles of cloth.

"Now class," Miss Pyle rose, making her way to the front of the room. "We will review the homework, then I will read the story of the 'Nightingale.' Please take out your lesson books and be ready. Oh, I'm sorry, Ruth, here is your lesson book. I'll explain about its use after class." She handed her a small, thin book with a black cover. On the front of the book was an empty, white space.

When Wind Flower glanced at the girl beside her, she saw that she had made some marks, like those in the reader, in the white space on her book. She had also drawn a picture of a girl and a tiny house in the background. Forgetting to listen to Miss Pyle, she started thinking of what she might draw in her white space. The girl's picture had many colors, pale green grass, bright blue sky, and the soft, black of the girl's hair. "Do you understand that, Ruth?"

Caught off guard, she had no idea what the teacher had been talking about, but didn't care. She had no intention of speaking anyway. "Don't worry. We'll go over everything after class. Now then, I think that's it. As always children, I expect careful study and extra care with your lettering. Perfect strokes, clean lines. We want something very special to show Mr. Rose on his next visit!

"Are we ready for the story?" She picked up a large, brown leather book and began speaking. She told the story of an emperor, a very important chief, and his nightingale, a tiny, brown bird with a beautiful song. As she listened, Wind Flower felt tears threatening to tumble out again. Sitting on the hard, wooden bench in her stiff, binding clothes, she felt just like the poor nightingale trapped in his gilded cage. When Miss Pyle finished reading she closed the book and looked up smiling. "I will read more of Anderson's tales to you as the year goes on, but this tale has always been one of my favorites.

"Class dismissed. Remember children—quiet in the hallways. Mr. Carlson and Miss Christina will be waiting in the dormitories. Have a pleasant rest and I'll see you at dinner. Ruth, please remain here, and Alice too."

The other children bustled out quietly until only Wind Flower and a short, plump girl with thick glasses and a red bow in her hair remained. "Now girls, let's get down to business. Ruth, I assume cannot read, and so our third reader will be much too difficult for her at first. Alice, I would like you to tutor her during the study periods, to get her started. I'll adjust your assignments accordingly, as you are so far ahead of the others anyway.

"We will begin with the Preprimer," she said, handing her a thinner book with the same brown and blue cover as the book she already possessed. "Alice, you will read and reread the first story to Ruth until she has it committed to memory. Then we will begin some word work. You will also practice all her lettering, every night in the lesson book. You may choose three words from the reader story each night to have her write, once she has mastered the individual letters. Is that clear?"

"Yes, Miss Pyle." Alice's voice was husky and deep. She spoke like a Washita and Wind Flower wondered what tribe she had come from and how long it had taken for her to speak thus.

"Thank you, Alice. You are dismissed. Here is a note for Miss Christina explaining your tardiness. And Alice, please look for Ruth at dinner. She needs your guidance."

"Yes, Miss Pyle. Bye," she nodded shyly, smiling at Wind Flower before departing.

"Now, Ruth, you and I have to get down to business. Have you ever tried reading?" She shook her head. "Well, don't worry, you'll pick it up fast. Most of our children are reading nicely after one semester with all the help they receive. And most come speaking only their heathen tongues. Since you already speak and understand English, you should make excellent progress."

Miss Pyle proceeded to explain about the marks in the book, which she called letters and words. These letters and words corresponded to spoken English, and it was they that told the tales the children had spoken. This explained the one voice. Then, the teacher opened the black lesson book. Unlike the reader, there were no marks on its pages. "This is where you will write, where you may tell stories and practice your letters." She took up a feather which she called a "quill" and dipped it into a bottle of black liquid. "Ink." Scratching it smoothly over the paper, she made four separate squiggles.

"R-U-T-H, Ruth. These marks say your name."

"My name is Wind Flower," she replied stubbornly, hoping the kind woman might make the marks to say it.

"Not anymore it isn't, my dear. I know this seems strange right now, but you'll get used to it. Now, I'd like you to try your name right here." She pointed to the space right under her marks and held out the quill. Wind Flower took up the pen and tried, but the ink fell in pools all over the clean white paper.

"You'll catch on with practice, don't worry. Alice will help you. She's my best pupil. Please watch her carefully."

She rose and handed Wind Flower the books, holding out a long, thin box and snapping open the lid to reveal a tray holding eight different colors of paint. A brush lay alongside the shiny saucers of hard paint in a grooved notch. "Do you like them?" she smiled, closing the lid and handing them to Wind Flower. "They're for your picture, on the lesson book cover. It is your most important assignment tonight. Please give it careful thought, so that you'll create something special. The painting becomes the permanent cover of the book so I ask my students to submit a practice drawing to me first, before they paint directly onto their book. Do you understand?"

Nodding, she fingered the smooth metal surface of the box as the teacher continued, "Good, then here is your practice paper. Put it inside your lesson book now where it won't get wrinkled.

You'll need to ask the study hall teacher for a small bottle of water to wet and clean your brush with. I believe we're all set. Come, I'll walk you back to the dormitory."

Miss Pyle brought her back to the narrow room full of beds where Miss Christina was waiting. "Shoes off," she barked, pointing first to her feet, then to the shoes of the other girls, lined neatly on the floor at the foot of their beds.

"You needn't mime, Chris. She understands English," Miss Pyle smiled. "I'll see you at dinner, Ruth. Have a good rest."

She stood watching Miss Pyle retreat, holding her books and box of paints, uncertain of what to do next. Suddenly her arm was twisted behind her back and she was thrust towards her bed. "Don't stand there gawking, you little animal. It's rest time."

Lying down on the bed, she closed her eyes as the others had already done, but could not sleep. Her mind swirled with the events of the past days.

When the rest time was over Miss Christina yelled, "Everyone up. Shoes on! Be sharp!" As Wind Flower turned to rise she gazed up at a tiny window above her bed. If she stood on tiptoes, she might be able to look out across the fields. Look but that was all. Even without standing on her toes, the thick metal bars were clearly visible. The whole building was one huge cage of all of them, tiny, brown nightingales trapped inside.

Suddenly, pain ripped through her head, as her hair was seized from behind. "I said, be sharp, you ignorant heathen. Get your shoes on." Throwing her to the floor, Miss Christina flung her shoes at her, hitting Wind Flower in the chest. She struggled, but without Miss Craven there to help with the lacing, it was impossible. She would surely have received another blow had the girl in the next bed not come to her rescue. "Here, I'll show you. Like this." With quick, nimble fingers she tied the laces and was standing at attention before Miss Christina glanced in their direction again.

"Martha, lead the girls to manners class. Shut up, the bunch of you. The younger ones are still resting." A tall, heavy-set girl emerged from the far end of the room and called, "This way" and they all followed dutifully behind.

As they passed through the younger girls' sleeping room she noticed Laughing Dove's bed was empty. She wanted to stop and search for her, but Miss Christina walked at the end of the line. Wind Flower kept her place, saying a silent prayer to the Wise Ones to keep her sister safe.

CHAPTER 8

Miss Christina led them to the front of the building, into a large room to the left of the front door. A row of chairs had been arranged to circle the room. "Be seated," she commanded, gesturing to those who did not understand. "This is the Green Room, the most elegant of our two parlors. The room across the hall, the Blue Room, is off limits to students, except on very rare occasions. Remember that—no students allowed in the Blue Room, or this room either for that matter, unless invited."

"Thank you, Christina. You may leave us now." Miss Wilson was seated in a high-backed chair, facing them. Wind Flower had failed to notice the headmistress' presence until the latter spoke, so rapt was she by her surroundings. Pale, green paper swirled with streaks of gold covered the walls and the furniture, all curly and carved, was fashioned of wood, the like of which she had never seen. Each chair was covered in a different shade of green, with patterns of flowers, birds and swirling shapes. There was a small, white piano trimmed in gold at the far end of the room and many tables of varying sizes, holding tiny china figures, glittering silver dishes and lamps of cut crystal.

As she gazed at one of the many paintings hanging on the walls—most of them portraits of people in stiff, uncomfortable clothes—she heard Miss Wilson's voice, first in a quiet tone, then more loud and insistent. "Ruth, I would like you to please stand, so that the other girls may know you. Ruth ... I know you can understand me."

Wind Flower stood, shyly scanning the faces around her. "Thank you, Ruth. You may sit. Now class, where were we? Oh yes, soup spoons."

She handed each of them a rounded spoon and began her lesson, demonstrating the correct way to sip one's soup. Wind Flower thought the whole thing silly. Washita spoons were difficult enough to hold, much less use backwards, and she felt sure that she'd spill the soup as she tilted the spoon back towards her mouth.

Relieved that the spoons held no liquid, Miss Wilson's next words brought fear to her heart. "And, why, do you ask, are we having this lesson today? Well, I'll tell you. At my request, Cook Dorothy has made some excellent soup for our supper. This way you may all practice your newly learned skill immediately. Practice makes perfect, I always say!

"I shall walk around, observing each and every one of you tonight at the evening meal. And, I expect you to set a good example for our younger students. Remember, it's all in the wrists. Mr. Morgan will be instructing the boys on this same technique. Let's show them that we know how it's done."

The rest of class was spent reviewing previous lessons. Each skill was demonstrated and then the new student was asked to try. They went through proper table setting, use of the knife and fork and the proper way to use a spoon for eating porridge and other more solid fare. "Remember girls, if the porridge is thin, you should eat it as you would soup. Careful wrists, delicate tilts."

Wind Flower muddled her way through the class feeling clumsy and stupid. She just couldn't seem to make her fingers work the Washita's small, dainty eating tools. She felt awkward and frustrated, particularly with the fork and spoon.

Also, the ordeal of dinner loomed ahead, giving her a nauseous, uneasy feeling. Not only must she force down the horrible tasting food, but now she was expected to use correct manners while doing it. And, she thought sadly, there was little chance that they'd be served a steaming bowl of turnip soup like Na'go's. Thinking about Na'go and her summer soup made Wind Flower ache with homesickness.

As if sensing her pupil's feelings, Miss Wilson added, "Ruth, of course we will make allowances for you these first weeks, don't worry. It takes everyone a while to catch on. As long as you make an effort, we are patient.

"And now girls, it's time for dinner. Shall we go?"

As they entered the hall, Wind Flower scanned the room searching the tables for her sister. Finally she spotted her seated in the middle of a row of younger girls. Her head was bowed, her face hidden. As she started towards her, the girl, Mary, who had helped her lace her shoes, whispered, "No, not that way. We sit over there. Come, I'll show you."

There was unmistakable warning in Mary's words, but Wind Flower pulled away, heading for Laughing Dove. She had to check on her, to see for herself if her little sister was all right. As she neared the table, Laughing Dove spied her, crying out and reaching her arms towards her sister. As she turned, Wind Flower saw the reason for her sister's bowed head. Across her swollen cheek a red, angry welt blazed. One of her eyes was blackened. Tears streamed down her face, splotched and raw from hours of weeping.

There was no time to speak. Not even time to ask why she'd been beaten or by whom. Hugging her gently, Wind Flower whispered her love even as sharp, clawing fingers reached from behind to tear her away. "So you want some of the same, do you? Come on, you little she-devil. I'll take care of you." As Wind Flower struggled to free herself, she heard Laughing Dove wailing behind her and glanced back to see Miss Annabelle with her arm around Laughing Dove's shoulders. She appeared to be comforting the child rather than punishing her and Wind Flower breathed a sigh of relief. Miss Christina hauled her to the door of the dining hall.

Upon reaching the door they found the way barred by Miss Wilson. "Christina, this is Ruth's first night with us. I think we can be lenient in this instance, don't you? After all, everything is new to her and naturally she misses her sister."

"This is my affair, Harriet. Don't interfere."

"I'm afraid I must insist, Christina. Your father has put me in charge and I would like Ruth at table with us this evening. Please let me have her and I'll see that she behaves. Thank you."

Hatred blazed in the other's eyes, but she released Wind Flower and stalked off to the teachers' table. Miss Wilson led her to a spot next to Mary and whispered, "Now behave my dear, please!"

When all was quiet Miss Wilson called, "All rise," and the entire dining hall rose to sing the same prayer to the Great One as had been sung at lunch. Before she could protest, Mary pulled her firmly to her feet. She sang directly at Wind Flower, her eyes pleading the new girl to learn the words, begging her to conform. As they sat down, Mary whispered, "We're not allowed to associate with the younger ones, except on Sundays after services. Then we have visiting hours. Be careful. They're very strict about it."

Wind Flower decided that later she would inquire further about this Sunday visiting, but for the present she gave herself over to the ordeal of eating. The soup although vile-smelling, proved edible and she managed to consume most of it without spilling. Fearing punishment should she not finish the soup, she started to lift her bowl to her lips intending to drink the last bit.

Mary nudged her, "Like this," she smiled, tipping her bowl and using her spoon to scoop up the last of her soup.

After dinner came study hall, during which Alice worked with her on her letters. A patient, careful teacher, Alice had her pupil reciting the entire alphabet in a very short time. Then she helped Wind Flower practice writing letters, a much more arduous task than saying them. She also helped her to write her name. When she asked Alice to write Wind Flower, her tutor frowned, whispering, "Oh no, it's not allowed. We'd get into terrible trouble!"

Halfway through the study time, Alice left her to attend to her own work. "You can use this time to paint your practice picture for your lesson book. Good luck!"

Wind Flower had thought about the cover and had decided what she would paint. At first, she had thought about painting White Deer, laughing, his toothless grin and sparkling eyes were so vivid in her mind. She missed the old healer terribly and she sat for a long while thinking about him. His gentle hands and kind eyes seemed to reach out to her from far across the land that separated them, comforting her and bringing her courage.

White Deer did not hunt. Old age and the loss of his leg had ended his days on the trail. His leg, along with his entire family and everything he loved had been left behind at Sand Creek. One day he had spoken to her of Sand Creek, saying that after that day he would never speak of it again. He kept his promise.

Wind Flower and the medicine man had just finished burying a child who had died of the white man's consumption and were kneeling by tiny piles of rocks covering the small bundle. The child was an orphan. All his family had gone before him, taken by the sickness. Now he journeyed to meet them with only White Deer and Wind Flower to see him into the spirit world. On that particular day, White Deer had forbidden the others to come for fear that they too would be afflicted.

"I will tell you something, my brave Flower," he began, his eyes grave and etched with sorrow. "I would like to unburden myself because after almost 22 years I must speak of this to someone. I have chosen you because you are strong and because you will not shrink from the knowledge, but will remember it with your heart and use it wisely. Our young people need to know of the past. We have shielded you for too long and for what? Does our life get better with the years under the white man's thumb? Do we prosper in this barren land he has ceded to us? Still I am sorry to inflict this horror on you my child, and to see the innocence which must fly in the face of it."

With this fearful introduction, White Deer went on. "It was not yet midday, and I was in the tent of Gray Bear. Young and strong, Gray Bear was away with a band of our warriors, attempting to learn the Washita's latest movements and demands. A new soldier chief had been installed at Fort Lyon, replacing our friend, Major Wynkoop. As much as any white man, we trusted the major, but his replacement, a Major Anthony, was unsettling to our leaders and they were wary and alert.

"As I said, I was in the tent of Gray Bear. His squaw was ill with fever and their only son had also succumbed. The poultices I had made seemed to be helping and they were looking brighter. Doe Song, the squaw of Gray Bear, was heavy with child, but young and very brave. She cared little about her own distress, but was frantic for Black Paw, her six-year-old son. Her daughter, Yellow Eyes, was well and assisted me as best she could. She was twelve years old at the time, a tall, thin, willowy child, with the lightest brown eyes I have ever seen. Already young braves were vying for her attentions, although she had not yet reached womanhood. She had been up all night with me, tending to her mother and brother, but still she would not rest. I finally ordered her to lie down. She obeyed reluctantly.

"No sooner had Yellow Eyes closed her eyes when the first signs of trouble reached our ears. I heard someone, maybe White Antelope, calling out, "Stop, stop," in the white man's tongue, and I wondered what he was about. Soon it was clear. Shots rang out and he called no more. White Antelope had lived for over seventy-five years and in an instant he was gone. Without pulling back the tent flap, I knew that he had been shot. I also knew with certainty that his death would not be the last.

"'Father, they are all around us,' Yellow Eyes called from the door of the tent. I gathered up Doe Song and the girl cradled her brother. We made our way out of the tent unsure of how to proceed. I was then 42, long past my prime as a warrior and my eyesight was poor even then.

"Our camp lay to the north of Sand Creek. The stream bed was almost dry and our water supply meager and tainted. We lay to the west of Black Kettle's tents. His camp was in the center and we looked to him for guidance. We had climbed a small rise and spied Black Kettle and a small band of his people in the distance standing in front of his tipi. Black Kettle held a white man's flag, a child beside him held the white flag of truce. They were in clear view of the soldiers, but the latter paid them no heed. The soldiers fired again and again. Although avoiding the band gathered around Black Kettle, they seemed intent on killing whoever else lay in their path.

"There were few men in the camp at the time, as most were away with the warriors scouting or hunting in the surrounding hills. What men there were seemed to be the soldiers' initial targets. Then they turned on the others. Women and children were shot as they fled, their screams piercing the air again and again as the soldiers advanced. We had determined to try and reach Black Kettle as the camp behind us was nearly overrun with soldiers. Looking back I saw Gray Bear's tipi in flames and many of our people lying dead on the cold, hard creek bottom.

"We were not far from Black Kettle's group when our way was blocked with a fresh contingent of soldiers. These men had brought up the rear and had not yet tasted blood. I knew the white man's tongue well by this time and I heard some of the officers enjoining their men to cease fire and spare the women and children. Their commands were heeded for a short time and we had a brief moment when the carnage abated. These troops, however, were soon joined and infected by those already drenched with the people's blood and their hearts and souls fled to meet the devil that drove their brothers.

"I pulled Yellow Eyes in a different direction. Even with my poor sight, the futility of our advancing farther was clear to me. Her soft eyes were wild with fright and her brother now cried and struggled in her arms. Doe Song implored me to leave her and run with the others, but I held fast to her suddenly aware that her child had chosen this time to come into the world. She closed her eyes against the pain and we headed south away from the firing.

"In a matter of minutes we were joined by many others fleeing alongside us and with our increased number came the attention of a renegade band of soldiers. They were upon us in seconds, howling and crying for death. We reached a small ravine that had once been a rippling stream. Now a small depression in the dry, cracked earth, scraggly brush grew beside it in a few spots offering protection from sight. I pushed Yellow Eyes down with Black Paw beneath her and their mother beside them. Endeavoring to shield them with my body, we had barely settled when the first round of fire hit us. I was struck immediately.

"A searing flame ripped through my thigh, but I lay still hoping they would pass by and leave those beneath me alone. I prayed for my death, if only that hers might be spared. Gray Bear had entrusted them to me and I was their only hope.

"The soldiers did not retreat, but kept firing, sending round after round into the ravine where many of us hid so ineffectually. The next volley to reach us was more intense and I waited for the death that must fall, lying still and silent, hoping to save the family of my old friend. I heard voices over me yelling, "That one still lives. For God's sake, finish him off. There are others getting away!"

"A hail of bullets struck my legs. Very bad aim, I remember thinking, as I lost consciousness from the pain and impact of the musket balls.

"It was much later, and growing dark, when I awoke. Little Elk, a boy of fourteen, was pulling at my sleeve, trying to force me up. I called out for him to stop, saying that I must protect Doe Song and her children when I spied a pitiable mass of flesh beside me.

At first, it looked like buffalo entrails and I was confused, imagining that I'd come upon a hunting party and was amidst the butchering that follows a kill. Then, my eyes and mind cleared and I saw that what I gazed upon was a baby, or what was left of a baby—Doe Song's unborn girl child, still encased in her embryonic sack. Beside her lay her mother, horribly mutilated after death. Not only had the soldiers slashed open her body, ripping the child from her womb, but they had scalped her as well. Her dignity had been trod upon, but not her delicate beauty. I touched her soft face, noticing a tear frozen on her cheek in the icy, winter air. I wanted to weep, but the shock of her death drove all tears from my heart.

"Everywhere around us lay women and children. Babies of friends and loved ones—they had been scalped and, like Doe Song, many of the bodies had been horribly mutilated. I looked for Gray Bear's children and found Black Paw close by, dead—a single shot through his forehead. Mercifully, he had not suffered. He, too, had been scalped, his young face, streaked with blood, now sleeping in death.

"We searched for many hours. We walked all through the camp, thankful for the growing darkness, that obscured some of the horror. Little Elk held me up, pulling me along, my useless left leg dragging behind. I would not let him rest till we'd searched everywhere. Still there was no sign of Yellow Eyes. The boy's back was strong and he held up well. All of his family was gone and I suspected he held on to me, dragging me about as if, through his labors, he might hold on to sanity amidst the unspeakable devastation surrounding us.

"After our search, we began the long march, struggling through the bitter cold to reach the warriors, camped 50 miles to the east. Among the dead left behind were the chiefs, White Antelope, One-Eye and War Bonnet. Black Kettle had eluded the soldiers, but his family had suffered heavy casualties. On the second day, I realized that we could carry my leg no farther. Instructing Little Elk in how to stop the bleeding, cleanse the wound and the proper way to chop into the bone, I gave the order and bit down on my knife handle. He raised his hatchet and I remembered no more. When I awoke, I was resting in a tent. The people were preparing for war, all other options having been laid to waste on the dry stream beds of Sand Creek.

"And that, Wind Flower, is how I lost my leg and whatever hope I had for my people. I lost three sisters and many kindred to the white man's guns that day and with them all that I held dear. My only solace came from the fact that I was childless, and had not the burden of mourning for my sons and daughters as so many others had.

"My wife Star Blanket had died in childbirth soon after we were married. After her death, I had no wish to marry again and have given my life to the healing. You see, we never had a healer, a medicine man or woman in the camp of my kindred. If there had been someone there, Star Blanket might have lived. Now I am glad she was taken. I'd have been powerless to save her at Sand Creek." His voice trailed off and White Deer was silent for some time. In the growing darkness as they headed to camp, Wind Flower asked, "And Yellow Eyes? Did you ever hear from her?"

"Yes," he replied, pain etched in every line of his face. "We heard news of her several moons later when those who had remained behind reached camp.

Travelers searching for survivors had ventured closer to the fort in the aftermath of the slaughter. It was on the outskirts of the open prairie, stretching towards the heavily guarded perimeter of Fort Lyons, where they found her. Yellow Eyes and several other young girls lay naked, their clothes ripped from them, and their bodies violated before death and mutilated afterwards. I was glad we hadn't found her. That way I could remember her as she lived, her soft tawny eyes, so full of wisdom and love, the gentle hands that tended her family with tireless care. Forever young, forever innocent.

"And now, Wind Flower, You have seen the only tears you will ever see me shed. It is a terrible burden I have placed upon you, but one I know you will use wisely. Remember the past, and hold on to the knowledge that no matter what the white man does to us, he can never steal our souls."

Returning to camp, Wind Flower had helped with the cooking as usual, but, many moons passed before she was able to return to life among the tribe. The pain and horror of the White Deer's tale had numbed her. She replied if spoken to, but otherwise remained silent, feeling half-dead among the living kindred that surrounded her.

Now as she settled into the harsh reality of Rose Academy, she felt the same numbness creeping over her. Finally, willing the sadness away, she took out her paint box and the stark white paper, ready to begin. She would not paint White Deer, but she felt certain that his hand would guide her.

CHAPTER 9

Miss Craven brought her a small jar of water and Wind Flower dipped the soft, thin brush first into the water and then to the circles of color in her box.

She had decided to paint Na'go, as her mother worked the buffalo hides. As the oldest daughter, she would someday receive her mother's knife, the knife used to work the hides, cut the meat and slice the strips of leather to dry in the sun.

Although Wind Flower hated the butchering and the blood, she wanted that knife and the symbolic power that it brought with it. Made many generations before, it was handed down from mother to daughter till it reached her Na'go. Expertly sharpened before the butchering began each season, it held its edge for many moons. Many of the women coveted the knife, proclaiming it the finest in the tribe and many had offered to trade for it but Na'go would never part with it. She kept it for her oldest daughter.

Although the shades of color in the box were quite different than the colors of the earth to which she was accustomed, Wind Flower was an experienced painter. She mixed and blended the paints with her brush, until she had just the right colors. Soon Na'go sprang from the paper, beautiful and tall, her hair, braided with feathers and brightly colored beads. For the butchering she would have worn little jewelry and no beads in her hair, but Wind Flower wanted to use all the colors in her box. Wanted to make her mother as beautiful as she was.

As the painting took shape Wind Flower felt better than she had since their capture. Seeing her beautiful mother before her, brought comfort and happiness. She was just adding Laughing Dove and herself to the picture, their shapes barely formed when Miss Craven called out, "Study Hall is over, boys and girls. Please pick up all your belongings and off to bed with you."

Hurrying by with her books, Mary whispered, "Don't worry if you're not finished. Miss Pyle will give you time at the beginning of class. She always does."

Wind Flower cleaned up the paints and Miss Craven showed her where to empty out the water. She carried the picture on top of her books, careful not to touch the still wet surface. Miss Craven accompanied her back to the dormitory, wishing her a good night at the door. "Just tell Miss Christina where you've been my dear. It will be fine."

As she walked away, Wind Flower entered the sleeping room alone. Many of the girls were already dressed in long, white sleeping gowns and as she reached her bed, she saw that a gown had been left out for her. Mary, already tucked into her bed whispered, "Quick, put on your nightgown. You're late!"

Shoving her things under the bed, and not bothering to remove her cumbersome undergarments, she was struggling into her nightgown when Miss Christina appeared out of nowhere. "Where have you been?"

When she didn't answer right away, the dorm mistress strode up, grabbing her by the hair. "I'm talking to you—you filthy animal. You're late. Where've you been?"

"Please, Miss Christina. She doesn't understand. She was painting her lesson cover in study and she had to clean up," Mary said, her voice quavering.

"Shut up and let her do her own talking. The little vermin understands me perfectly. Now where were you? Think you're Miss Wilson's little pet, do you? Well, she's not here now to protect you, is she? I'll show you who's really in charge."

The hatred in her eyes silenced Wind Flower and she stared at the floor, praying that the horrible woman would go away. "And what have we been painting?" As she reached for the painting, Wind Flower tried to grab it, but Miss Christina struck her hard across the side of her face and she fell across the bed, dazed. As she stared at the painting, the dorm mistress' face turned from pasty white to deep crimson. For an instant Wind Flower thought she glimpsed a smile flicker in the cold eyes.

Then, the smile disappeared and the dorm mistress screamed, "Blasphemy!" ripping the paper to shreds. "I should have whipped you when I had the chance. You savages don't learn anything unless it's pounded into you."

She grabbed Wind Flower's nightgown, dragging her from the room down the hall to her bedroom. There Wind Flower was stripped of her nightgown and thrown across a wide stuffed chair face down. Before she could rise to defend herself, she felt the lash across her back.

Again and again she struck, shoving Wind Flower down each time she tried to rise. Each time the lash descended, Miss Christina repeated the words, "You have no past. Your life begins now," over and over again. Finally she stopped and tore Wind Flower's undergarments off, dragging her across the room naked and nearly unconscious from pain and fright.

As she pulled her along, one hand squeezed Wind Flower's left breast so hard that she cried out. Laughing, Miss Christina let go, throwing the nightgown over her head and yanking it down. As she backed away, Wind Flower saw that the front of the dorm mistress' dress was stained red with blood.

She took a wobbly step towards the door, hoping the torture was over. "Oh no, you don't," she snarled. "You're spending the night right here." Laughing again, she opened a door and thrust Wind Flower into an empty closet, slamming the door. "There! And not a peep out of you or there'll be more of the same."

Wind Flower lay down on the cold, hard floor and wept silently. Her back throbbed as the harsh cloth of the nightgown rubbed against her skin, clinging to the open, oozing wounds. Finally, she fell into a painful, half-sleep from which she remembered nothing till the door opened the following morning.

CHAPTER 10

Just before sunrise, the door of her dark prison was opened and Wind Flower was dragged out and unceremoniously dumped into her bed. Darkness blanketed the sleeping room, but the Wise Ones Above sent faint fingers of dawn's light through the bars of the window above the bed. The dancing sun beams gave her courage despite her pain and fear of what the day would bring. "See that you stay quiet," her tormentor hissed, her bare feet soundlessly retracing the steps to her own room.

Curling up under the scratchy blanket, Wind Flower tried to sleep, but she hurt all over and her mind was a whirl of confusion and pain.

Just after sunrise Miss Christina came to wake them, "All up," she called, approaching Wind Flower's bed. "Get your things," she snarled. "You'll dress in my room so I can check to see you do it properly."

When Wind Flower hesitated, afraid of another beating, she said "All the new girls dress for me the first day. Now hurry up." Throwing a blanket over her victim's shoulders, the dorm mistress bustled her hastily from the room, pushing her ahead of her along the corridor. As they went, Wind Flower heard a voice calling the others to breakfast. It sounded like the woman called Miss Craven, but she couldn't be sure.

Wondering at the dorm mistress' sudden act of kindness in giving her the blanket, Wind Flower found that the charity lasted only until the door was shut to the other's room. There the warm covering was torn from her back, her nightgown following it. Arrows of pain shot down her back as the raw, crusted wounds pulled away from the cloth.

"I'll take care of this filth," the dorm mistress said, throwing the bloody nightgown on the floor. She gave Wind Flower a scratchy undershirt without sleeves to wear under her dress. "And keep it on at night too," she snarled, "Just put your nightgown over it."

With the extra layer she felt even more trapped in her new clothes. The weather was still very warm in the Moon When the Deer Paw the Earth (September) and her body felt as though it were roasting over an open fire under the layers of cloth.

Leading her back to the dorm to retrieve her shoes and books, Miss Christina then delivered her to breakfast. Wind Flower glimpsed Laughing Dove at her place across the room and managed a covert smile. Her sister looked a little better except for the bruises on her face. Tired, puffy eyes told her that Laughing Dove had not slept. She needed her older sister to sing her to sleep. Someone had combed her hair, Wind Flower noticed. What little there was of it had been brushed smooth. Instead of looking coarse and wiry as her own did, her sister's hair looked soft and shiny and Wind Flower wondered who had given her such special care. The other new children looked as she did, their hair stiff and matted down from the fire water baths.

As she neared her table, she heard a voice calling softly, "Ruth, come sit by me!" Looking up she spied Mary smiling and patting a space beside her on the bench. Grateful for the other's kindness and her efforts to intervene on her behalf the previous evening, Wind Flower smiled back and whispered "Thank you."

"You can speak. I thought so," she whispered back, careful to keep her eyes to the front. The Washita Great One's song was sung after which they were each served a bowl of watery grain. "Eat," Mary whispered, "It's the best meal of the day."

The cereal had little taste, but was easier to swallow than the hash. She ate slowly, trying to use her spoon the way Miss Wilson had taught them. Several times the spoon sprung from her hands, once skittering across the floor before

Mary, again her rescuer, bent to retrieve it. Despite her mistakes, Wind Flower was left alone. No one leapt forward to chastise her lapses in table manners and she managed to finish her bowl in relative peace.

After breakfast, they went to chapel. A separate building, the chapel was a short walk across an open field behind and to the north of the main building. A small structure, its walls were fashioned of stone and mud. Around the perimeter flowers bloomed in carefully tended beds, red, purple and white blossoms peeked out from amidst a sea of green. At the peak of the low roof a Washita cross, golden in the morning sunlight, reached up towards the blue sky. Inside the building the air was cool and light streamed in from the tall windows on either side of the sanctuary. They sat on hard benches with low backs, eight students to a row.

When everyone had entered, every other person reached to a rack on the back of the bench in front of them, opening a thick, red book, she would later learn was called a hymnal. All rose except the newcomers, who quickly followed suit. They sang a song to the Great One, then sat again. After several announcements from Miss Craven, Miss Wilson spoke to them about truth and the importance of honesty.

The white man's truth, not ours, Wind Flower thought sadly, bowing her head, blinking back tears. A truth that condoned broken promises and ignored treaties. A truth that forced the people to live on tiny reservations on barren land while the fertile land and rich hunting grounds were given to the ever-increasing bands of white settlers that migrated west. It was a truth that brought disease and starvation to the people. A truth that had robbed her of her life.

When the talk was finished the headmistress asked for silence, beseeching them to speak in their own words to the Washita Great One. A welcome respite, this period of silence was to become Wind Flower's most treasured time of the day. As many moons passed in the prison called Rose Academy, she would look forward to the precious moments of silence, of release from the oppression of her days. No matter what she suffered the rest of the time, during silence Wind Flower was free to return home. Free to hug Na'go and run through the woods with Laughing Dove. Free to ride Water Eyes with her long braids flying behind her, the wind cutting into her face till it brought tears. Tears of happiness and freedom. Silence. She had found one Washita custom that she liked.

After the time of quiet, they filed out of the chapel room in lines, each group dispersing to collect their books and go on to their classrooms. Mary and Alice led her back into the low building at the rear, entering a different classroom than Miss Pyle's. There a round, pudgy little man no taller than herself awaited them. "Well, well, I see we have a new recruit. Step right up little lady and let me take a look. Name?"

When there was no reply Mary said, "Her name is Ruth, Mr. Morgan, and she can speak English, but she's very shy."

"Well, is that a fact? A bit on the shy side, is she? I'm a bit like that myself. I'm sure we'll get along just fine." Winking at her, he motioned Wind Flower to an empty seat in the front row. "Sit right here, Ruth. That way you won't miss nothing and I can keep my eye on ya. Long as you can do yer sums there'll be no need for talk right away. When you're more comfortable you can show us all up."

The man called Morgan had kind eyes and a warm smile. She wondered why she hadn't seen him at meal time, certain that she'd have noticed him at the teachers' table with his bright yellow vest and red bow tie.

Struggling through her first mathematics class, understanding little of what was said, she found the science class that followed much more to her liking. They were studying plants native to the area and Mr. Morgan explained that they would be hiking in the nearby woods looking for specimens.

Mr. Morgan showed them beautiful prints of plants and flowers mounted on stiff, cream-colored paper. She recognized many of the plants, marveling at the artist's ability to capture them so vividly. Mr. Morgan seemed to have little interest in or knowledge about the names of the plants. He simply wanted the students to identify them by name.

How disgusted White Deer would be, she thought smiling to herself, were he listening to this Washita rambling on. The idea of collecting and identifying plants, then discarding them, particularly the plant that Mr. Morgan called "sweet pine," would have been too much for White Deer to bear!

Very rare around the Tongue River country, the sweet pine plant, wi us kimohk shin, was highly prized. Young girls from puberty to marriage wove it into pillows and braves used it to perfume their favorite horses. How excited the people would be if she brought back some "sweet pine!"

"After our botanical study," Mr. Morgan concluded, "we'll begin our study of the animal life in the area. Now then, that's it for today. Any questions?" His bright eyes darted about the room, inviting and ready to help, but no one raised a hand. "Very well. You know the assignment for tonight. I'll see you in the morning."

As they rose, preparing to depart, Mr. Morgan called, "Ruth, please stay for a moment. And Mary, you too. Then you can guide our Ruthie to lunch safely. Here, come and sit. I won't bite you."

Sitting where he directed, she listened as he explained a little of what the class had been studying. "You're a lucky one, my dear. We've just come back from summer break. Much less catch up for you. Why you only missed two weeks. Mary here'll help you, won't you Mary?" Mary nodded and smiled.

"We have mathematics every day. You'll pick it up; probably have the basic idea in that Indian head of yours already. 'Course I know, you're just startin' out, but I'd bet you're a quick study. Sure look like a smart one to me. Lots going on behind those cornflower blue eyes, I'll wager."

She longed to speak, to tell him her real name. She wanted to explain that she had been named for the prairie cornflower, the same flower depicted so realistically on his shiny hard paper, but instead she sat silently listening. She had long since learned that cruelty lurked behind smiles in the world of the Washita. Cruelty and pain.

"Now then, where was I? Ah yes—science classes are held on Tuesdays and Thursdays. Mondays and Fridays we take up our geography studies and then Wednesday you're off with Cook for some kind of thingamobobby. Cooking, I guess she calls it," he winked, patting her knee.

"So, Ruthie, have you any questions, before I release the two of you?"

When his question elicited only silence, he went on, "Not to worry—they'll come. Questions always do, eventually. Curiosity will get the better of you, just wait and see.

"Here," scribbling on a piece of paper, he handed it to Mary. "Give this to Miss Wilson. If she's not in the dining hall yet, give it to Craven. Explains your tardiness."

Patting her gently on the shoulder, he was startled to see his new pupil recoil as if his very touch had wounded her. Try as she might, Wind Flower could not keep her expression neutral. The pain was excruciating. "Sorry, darlin'—hey, it's okay! Didn't I tell you I don't bite! Now scoot the both of you."

Gathering their things, the girls departed. Mr. Morgan did the same, but headed off in the opposite direction. "Mr. Morgan lives in town," Mary explained as they walked slowly to lunch.

"He only comes out for morning classes, then goes home till it's time for the boys' manners class. His wife won't live at school 'cause she's sickly and is afraid to be too far from her doctor. We're lucky to have him. He and Miss Pyle are the nicest teachers in the school. I know, I've had 'em all."

"How long have you been here?" Wind Flower asked.

"Five years," the other replied. "Since I was eight. I'm Nez Perces, or I was, from the tribe of Chief Joseph. My brother and I were taken together from the Lapwal after the tribe separated. Our chief was sent into exile, my parents were both dead and we were starving. It was no trouble for the men to take us from my old grandmother's tent by the river. She was ill with the white man's sickness and very weak. I had no time to call out, no time to say good-bye. I'm sure by now she has gone to join the Great Spirits. She was very old then and for many moons she had begged the Wise Ones to take her.

"Have you and your brother tried to escape?"

"My brother is dead. He died in my arms, of the fever, the morning of our arrival. We came in winter and the fire water room was very cold and he was so weak … After he was taken there was no one left but me, no place for me to go. No one for me to …" Tears welled up in her eyes. She brushed them away quickly, her eyes darting all around to make certain they were alone.

Wind Flower took her hands and for a moment they walked in silence. As they neared the end of the corridor, Mary whispered, "We mustn't speak of the time before. Not ever! Miss Christina likes nothing better than to catch us talking of the old ways. It's an excuse for a beating."

Lunch proved a simple meal of bread and fruit. The bread, stale and moldy around the edges was nonetheless edible and there were no utensils to fuss with. Wind Flower noticed that Miss Christina seemed to be avoiding her. Silently thankful for whatever force kept the cruel dorm mistress at bay, she dared to approach her sister's table at the end of the meal.

There was just time for a quick hug before Miss Craven gently separated them. Laughing Dove's chubby arms and clinging fingers sent shivers of pain down her back as the child clung desperately to her. Refusing to flinch, so happy was she to be near her beloved sister, Wind Flower bore the pain in silence.

"Sunday visiting hours, girls. That 's the time for seeing friends." As she pried them apart, Wind Flower kissed the soft, wet cheek, whispering, "I'll find you tonight little one. Be brave." As Laughing Dove was led away by Miss Annabelle, her older sister wondered if perhaps it was the attentive Miss Annabelle who had combed Laughing Dove's hair so carefully.

Barely seated in her afternoon class, Miss Pyle approached her, asking how she was getting on. Alice raised her hand and volunteered, "She's ever so smart, Miss Pyle. Her lettering will be fine once she gets the feel of the quill. She already knows all her letters. Ask her and she'll write 'em for you. Her name too."

"Thank you, Alice. You are an excellent teacher. I can see you'll have our Ruth reading in no time. Now then my dear," she smiled, leaning over the desk, "Let's take a look at your lessons." She praised the lettering, pronouncing Alice an excellent teacher again. "Very satisfying night's work I'd say. We'll plan some further work for you after class."

Class proceeded much as it had the previous day with lettering practice and reading. Once again, at the end of class Miss Pyle sat down to read from the heavy book by the man called Anderson. "Hans Christian Anderson lived in Denmark. You will learn about the country of Denmark in Mr. Morgan's geography class. The story I will read today is called 'The Little Mermaid.'"

This story concerned a girl that lived under the sea. Instead of legs she had the tail of a fish. Having never seen the sea, Wind Flower could only imagine its size and the things called waves rising up like mountains in the churning waters of the storm. Wind Flower marveled as she

listened, marveled at the brave, little mermaid's sacrifice made out of love for the prince. Miss Pyle explained in a low voice that a prince was like the son of a great Indian chief.

Wind Flower's heart ached at the tale's end. Ached for the mermaid as she dissolved into foam, unable to return to her people and forsaken by the stupid prince. She didn't understand why the man called Anderson would write such an unhappy tale.

As if echoing her thoughts, Miss Pyle said, "Hans Christian Anderson wrote many stories. Like the 'Nightingale' and 'The Little Mermaid,' many of them have sad endings, but they are beautiful nonetheless. They stir our hearts and allow us to feel deeply for their unique and courageous characters." Wind Flower found herself agreeing with Miss Pyle—her heart felt the pain of Mr. Anderson's characters almost as if it were her own.

After the others were dismissed, Alice waited while Miss Pyle gave her new pupil the evening's assignment. "Now dear, do you understand? Wind Flower nodded. "Good. Now let's see your practice sketch for your lesson book cover. Did you have a chance to work on it?"

Alice opened her mouth as if to speak, but closed it again, not daring to speak against Miss Christina. Alice's words were unnecessary, however, as Wind Flower's face betrayed her feelings yet again. She bowed her head as unbidden tears streaked down her cheeks.

"Oh, my. What's happened?"

As Wind Flower cried, Alice blurted out the entire story. Of the beautiful drawing torn to shreds, of the dorm mistress' dragging Wind Flower away. Alice related everything she knew, but of course she knew nothing of the beating or the closet.

"Oh Ruth, I am sorry. It was partially my fault, I'm afraid. I thought you'd been sufficiently warned. No more of your old ways. You must try to forget your past, please dear, for your own good. You see that it only gets you into trouble. Here now, I'll give you a fresh paper and you can make a new picture tonight. Take the box of paints with you again. Does that make you feel better?" With these words she reached over to straighten the collar of Wind Flower's dress.

In so doing she noticed the top hem of the scratchy undershirt. "Good heavens, what's this?" An undershirt on a hot day like this?" she said, reaching in, to pull on the strap. Wind Flower screamed as the cloth pulled away from her wounds.

Turning to Alice, Miss Pyle almost whispered, "Alice. You may go to manners class. I will escort Ruth myself. Run along dear. I'll explain to Miss Wilson later on. Go on now!"

Closing the door, she beckoned to Wind Flower. "Come here dear. Don't be afraid. I just want to look at your back. I promise I'll be very careful." Gently she eased the dress over her shoulders. Careful as she was, every movement sent shivers of pain through Wind Flower and she gripped the bench, biting her lips to keep from crying out. Finally, the undershirt was peeled away as Miss Pyle cried out, "Lord help us!

"Wait here, dear," she said, already halfway out the door. "Don't be afraid. I'll lock the door. No one will see you. Do you understand?" Wind Flower nodded. Miss Pyle disappeared, returning a short time later with Miss Wilson and the woman called Nurse.

The headmistress looked at Wind Flower's back, saying little, but instructing the nurse to administer to her at once. While Nurse rubbed salve on the wounds, afterward applying a cloth dressing, the others spoke softly across the room. Unable to make out their words, she could nonetheless see the agitation on Miss Pyle's face. The headmistress' face revealed nothing.

After she'd been helped back into her dress, minus the undershirt, Miss Wilson said, "Now ladies, kindly leave us."

When the others had departed, she said, "Did Miss Christina do this to you?" Wind Flower nodded.

"Where did this beating take place? Come, come child, your silence hurts only you in this instance. Was it in her room?" She was answered with a nod once again.

"Did you spend the night in Miss Christina's room?"

Another nod.

"I see," she sighed. "All right, that will be all. Come along with me to what remains of our manners class. And, please, for goodness' sake, do try to forget your past. As this episode has clearly illustrated, it brings nothing but trouble."

Following Miss Wilson, Wind Flower was glad she hadn't spoken. No matter what happens, Washita protect each other, she thought bitterly. No, she would not speak to this woman who by her very words condoned the punishment meted out by Miss Christina.

CHAPTER 11

Free of the scratching undershirt, her wounds dressed and bandaged, Wind Flower felt more comfortable. Without the extra layer of coarse, bristling fabrics, the dress and pinafore seemed light and airy and as the sun's fire cooled, she felt almost happy. For a few fleeting minutes, she forgot about her prison and imagined herself free again, running along the banks of the Tongue.

Dinner was served cold on account of the heat. Bowls of cold hash, mixed with chopped, boiled potatoes had already been set at each place. The potatoes dulled the taste of the putrid rotting flesh, making the hash easier to swallow. She chewed slowly, imagining that she sat before a bowl of Na'go's red turnip stew and was able to clean her plate without gagging.

Again Alice helped her in study hall, leaving some time for her to work alone. Mathematics proved much easier than reading. Wind Flower was well-used to counting and figuring; only the squiggly lines on the flat, white paper seemed strange and new.

Wind Flower slipped the white paper from her lesson book and opened her paint box. Before she could rise to ask, Miss Craven appeared with a cup of water. Wind Flower had already decided what she would paint. If she must paint a white man's picture, she would make the chapel house and the flowers that bloomed all around it.

Choosing her colors carefully, she closed her eyes, recalling the purple, white and golden shapes of the flowers. Mixing and experimenting until she had just the right hues, she made fine,

delicate lines, building the chapel house stone by stone, until it appeared fully formed on the heavy white paper. She even painted the cross on its roof reaching up to the sky.

She knew that the cross was a symbol for the Great One the Washita call God, but this painting was a silent prayer to the Wise One of her people, who dwelt in the sky. In her mind, the cross reached up, from her heart to his, but no one need know that. She would let the teachers think her the good Christian Miss Wilson admonished them all to be.

Interspersed among the flowers surrounding the chapel, she painted tiny flowers that grew in the fields near the Tongue River Reservation. They blended right in, highlighting the beauty of the cultivated plants and she hoped that no one noticed them for what they were, reminders of the world her captors sought to eradicate.

Finally, in a few defiant brush strokes, she painted Water Eyes, her pony, half hidden in the woods beside the chapel. Wild ponies were common throughout the region and would not look out of place in the picture. Smiling at her cunning, she set back and admired her work, drawing strength and courage from the tiny painting. Emblazoned on the lesson book used every day these secret reminders of home would help to stave off the loneliness until she could go home.

When Miss Craven called "Bedtime children," she lifted the completed picture from the desk, blowing softly over its suffice to dry it. Mary came up behind her, exclaiming, "Oh Ruth, it's beautiful. Wait till Miss Pyle sees it!"

Sullen and aloof, Miss Christina continued to ignore her as the children dressed for bed. A clean nightgown lay on her bed and as she slipped into it, several of the girls murmured about the bandages. Noticing the disturbance, the dorm mistress screamed, "Get into bed, the lot of you and quit your gawking!" Turning on her heels, she stalked out of the room, the hard, clicking footsteps echoing along the corridor's bare wood floors.

The night sounds lulled her companions to sleep, but Wind Flower lay awake, waiting. After a time, she rose, creeping towards the room where her sister slept. A closed door separated the rooms, but it was unlocked. Opening it slowly, with care, lest it squeaked and gave her away, she stole noiselessly into the next room.

Her night eyes were sharp and well-trained and she had no difficulty locating Laughing Dove's bed. The tiny body lay tense and watchful in the middle of the bed and Wind Flower smiled, knowing her sister was fully awake, waiting for her. She lowered herself slowly onto the cot, slipping her arms around the trembling child. Immediately Laughing Dove's body heaved with sobs as she collapsed against her older sister. "Hush, little one. I cannot stay if you cry. They'll hear us. Shush!"

Afraid of losing the comforting presence, Laughing Dove quieted, resting her head on Wind Flower's shoulder. The tiny chest relaxed and her breathing became more regular. "I will sing very softly, my sister," she whispered, "but in my heart I will shout the words so you must listen carefully."

As she sang the rolling, rollicking story of the bear lumbering through the forest bringing food to his little ones, Wind Flower felt her sister's body soften against her own. After a few lines she paused to ask if Laughing Dove had heard and she nodded, sniffling as they nestled closer together.

Near the end of her song, her sister's slow, steady breathing told her that she slept. She stayed a little longer, holding her, comforted by the smooth, soft cheek against her own. Despite Miss Christina's fire water and stinging washes, she still smelled like Laughing Dove, her hair, her skin and her breath—cool, sweet, baby's breath like a mountain brook in early spring.

Except for the bruises on her face, Laughing Dove appeared to be healthy and well-cared for. Someone seemed to be tending to her with particular care and attention. Pangs of jealousy jabbed at her heart and Wind Flower chided herself, knowing that she should be grateful to whoever was caring for her sister. And, she was grateful. During Sunday visiting hours, she would inquire about the secret benefactor to whom she must feel such gratitude.

CHAPTER 12

During her first year at Rose Academy, Wind Flower made two attempts to escape—the first only a short time after their arrival. For the first try, she saved crusts of bread from each meal and fruit too. Beyond that she had made no other preparations. She hadn't told Laughing Dove of her plans, fearing the child would give them away.

As usual Wind Flower went to her sister at bedtime, but the night of the escape, instead of singing, she had grabbed her sister's clothes, clapped her hand over her mouth, and hastily explained where they were going. Laughing Dove struggled, fearing the punishment should they be caught, but eventually she quieted.

They dressed quickly and Wind Flower led the way, their supplies slung over her shoulder. The tiny figures stole silently across the grounds, dwarfed by the brick giant, the building gazing down at them with unseeing eyes, asleep like its occupants. Although the moon was full, they were soon swallowed up in the inky blackness of the woods at the edge of the grounds. As they traveled farther away, the towers of the school disappeared and their spirits lifted.

It felt good to be free walking hand in hand. Hungry already, Laughing Dove was assuaged by the shiny red apple her sister handed her. Confident that she could forage for food along the way, Wind Flower's main difficulty lay in discovering which way to go. Mr. Morgan's geography class had taught her that thanks to the

Iron Horse they were a long way from home, but she had learned little else about the land between Rose County and Tongue River.

"My feet are tired," Laughing Dove whined after less than an hour of walking. She dragged her along for a time but then Wind Flower was forced to take the child up onto her back. Walking all night, she carefully skirted the town, intending to find a sleeping spot with the sunrise, but as it turned out they never needed a place to sleep.

The trackers found them just before dawn and they were back at school by the start of the morning classes, confined in the small, dark punishment rooms in the cellar.

The punishment rooms had no furnishings save small, straw-filled mattresses and blankets. The three rooms were similar and Wind Flower came to know them all as well as the characters woven into her Na'go's wedding blanket. The damp, stone walls had one tiny window, high up. Too high to look out. A thin shaft of light filtered down through the thick, cobwebbed panes into the tiny cell below. Just enough light to grope one's way from one corner of the room to another.

Even if they could have done so, children were not permitted to study or read in the punishment rooms. They were to do nothing, but sit and think about their wrongdoing.

At first, it was frightening, but as time went by, punishment became simply boring and uncomfortable. The room was always cold and the dampness seeped into her till she was often left swimming in a sea of tears and shivering sweat.

She cried out again and again that it had been her fault, that Laughing Dove had been dragged along, against her will, but to no avail. They locked her sister up in one cell, two doors away from hers and Wind Flower could hear her cries of terror throughout the day and well into the night. When at first she'd called back to Laughing Dove, reassuring her, Miss Christina had flown in and bound and gagged her. After that she could only listen to her sister's wails, powerless to help, her heart breaking at the pain she had brought her. Finally, one day she heard rustling and the cries stopped. Laughing Dove had been let out of punishment.

Wind Flower remained in confinement through two more moons, into the cold nights of the Freezing Moon (November). Her food was thrown at her feet three times a day, her only human contact the hand that tossed in the food. She spent most of her time planning her next escape. There would be a great deal to learn before they'd be ready again.

One of the last days of her punishment, Miss Wilson came in to the cell. She brought a chair and sat looking down at the prisoner crouched on the filthy, straw mattress. Her lantern's light nearly blinded Wind Flower after living so long in the dark.

The headmistress stared at her for several minutes, breaking the silence with, "Ruth, what are we going to do with you?" As her query elicited no response, she continued. "My dear, don't you realize how lucky you are? Why, for every child that we rescue from savagery, there are hundreds of others who will never be saved. When you graduate from Rose Academy you will have opportunities beyond your wildest dreams. The graduates of Rose Academy are well known. My girls are sought after from all over the country as governesses, household employees and sometimes even teachers. But, they have to work hard to achieve success. I can furnish the education and a healthy environment for you, but you must do the rest. Do you understand me?"

"My name is Wind Flower and I want to go home."

"Defiant still. A pity... I'm sorry, my dear. You have had a long time to think here, yet your confinement does not seem to have brought you to your senses. I suggest you use these last few days to think of ways you might change, for the better."

When she walked out of punishment two days later, Wind Flower found her sister had become a stranger, lost to her as completely as if she had died. The first few nights she went to her sister's bed to sing and hold her, but instead of welcoming her, Laughing Dove struggled and fought, pushing her away. Then one night she found her sister's bed empty and the following Sunday she was informed that her sister now slept in Miss Annabelle's room. It was Miss Annabelle who sang her to sleep, Miss Annabelle who comforted her, Miss Annabelle who loved her and took care of her.

She warned, she begged and she pleaded, but it was no use. A wall of thorns, like the impenetrable thicket surrounding Briar Rose in Miss Pyle's fairy tale book, had sprung up between them. Laughing Dove loved Miss Annabelle now, not her sister. The pair took walks together, had tea together and went on outings into the town. Laughing Dove returned from these excursions loaded down with treats, candy, small trinkets and colorful drawing paper.

During Sunday visiting hours, Laughing Dove attempted to pass some of her treasures onto her sister, but Wind Flower refused the gifts, angrily throwing them to the ground. Soon her younger sister avoided her completely and spent her Sundays in private with her beloved Miss Annabelle.

As time went by Laughing Dove grew tall and slender, but her cheeks remained round and full. Her hair, unlike the rest of the pupils, was allowed to grow longer because Miss Annabelle had personally undertaken responsibility for its care. Instead of braids, her sister's hair was curled, like the hair of Washita girls, pulled back from her face with large ribbons.

From afar, Wind Flower watched sadly as time passed and her sister grew up. Although their estrangement ate away at her heart, she ceased her interference. Miss Annabelle was good to Laughing Dove. She protected her and looked out for her. Her sister was never beaten and was given the best food and extra treats that kept her healthy and well-nourished. And, Miss Annabelle was kind. At first, she tried to make friends, but hurt and jealous Wind Flower rebuffed the attempts at kindness. Eventually, she too gave up, contenting herself with lavishing affection on her protégé.

During the following summer in the Moon When the Cherries are Ripe (August), Wind Flower made her second escape attempt.

During the summer vacation months, the older children worked the fields of the surrounding towns as cheap labor for the farmers. The school, and more specifically the Rose family, were compensated for their students' labor. The children received nothing, save tired limbs and torn, raw flesh on hands and arms from harvesting the sharp stalks of grain in the endless fields that stretched for miles around the school.

As she worked, Wind Flower often watched the carts running back and forth along the road to town. From geography classes and listening to talk, she knew this road led to the railroad station from whence they had come. She thought she might catch a ride, unobserved in one of the carts, and waited for her opportunity.

They had been studying the surrounding territories in geography class that spring. On Mr. Morgan's maps, Tongue River looked to be about a five or six day ride from Rose County. She knew she must make the journey alone. Laughing Dove would never agree to accompany her. She was now Rachel, a Washita girl, frightened of the savage Indians she heard about in her social studies classes.

One day, Wind Flower found herself out of sight of the others just as a cart laden with farm equipment appeared over the rise. Inching her way slowly to the edge of the road, she crouched unseen until the cart rumbled past. Leaping up she grabbed hold of the wooden slats on the side of the cart. Splinters stabbed into her hands, but ignoring the pain, she hurled herself onto the cart, bruising her shin on the blade of a plow.

Resting for an instant to catch her breath, she glanced back. She had not been seen. Putting an oily, green cloth over her, she leaned back, peeking out of a hole from time to time to survey her surroundings.

They traveled briskly, covering the distance in good time. During the ride, the cart passed many people, some of whom waved and called out greetings to the driver. Hidden under the tarp, Wind Flower passed by unseen. The rolling hills eventually gave way to cool, green woods. Finally the driver turned onto the dusty, well-traveled road into town and Wind Flower sat up, realizing she must not ride all the way into the town in the cart.

Jumping off, she scrambled into the bushes at the side of the road. Slowly, she made her way towards the train station, careful to stay in the shadows, out of sight. She arrived shortly after the farmer and watching from behind a stack of old poultry crates, she waited, listening and hoping to learn the destination of the huge, black Iron Horse that loomed like a black puffing giant on the nearest tracks. Inching closer, she readied herself to leap onto the train as it pulled away.

Suddenly a man rode up shouting, "We got a runaway Jack! Out from the Academy. Bill Cotter spotted her jumpin' out the back of yer wagon as you came into town."

"Twern't there when I started out," the man replied. "Must of hopped in along the way."

"Likely she's headed for the train. Miss Wilson says she's a smart 'un. Probably fixin' to head out on the next train. Keep an eye out! I'll be back with the sheriff and some men in a minute. Old Mr. Rose pays a hefty bounty fer his runaways. Somethin' in it fer you if you spot 'er."

"What's she look like?"

"Tall, light skinned, light eyed. Fifteen. Probably still wearin' her blue school duds. Good luck. I'll be back. Name's Ruth."

Her heart pounding, Wind Flower tried to remain calm. If they began searching the grounds of the station, they'd discover her immediately. Inching back, she decided to run for the woods, perhaps catching the train down the line a ways.

"Hey, little lady. What's the rush?"

He grabbed her arm, holding tight. "Hank's the name, and I'm sorry but I ain't lettin' ya go. Miss Harriet'll pay me a tidy little sum fer you. 'Sides honey, you're better off with her doncha know that by now? Come on, none of that kicking now!"

Ignoring his words, she struggled, kicking and scratching, but to no avail. His grip was fast as he dragged her along as if she were but an old, dead tree limb he was clearing off his land. After a while she gave up and walked quietly at his side. She was caught, struggling would do no good. Reaching his horse, he mounted and pulled her up beside him, heading out of town. He called to the others as he rode by, telling them to call off the search.

As they made their way back, he endeavored to draw her into conversation but efforts were greeted with silence. She had no wish to speak to this man who transported her so cheerfully back to prison.

As they neared the gate, she shrank down in the saddle, leaning against him, closing her eyes, forcing back the tears that threatened to fall. "Hey now. It taint that bad now, Ruthie. I know yer name's Ruth. They told me at the sheriff's. I got a little gal 'bout yer age at home. You'd get along right well I expect. Too bad she's so far away. Her and her Ma moved back east till I can make money enough to buy us a farm.

"Well, here we are. Down ya go. Now don't you fret none. I'll see they don't punish ya. See if Hank don't."

And Hank did see to it. For a second escape attempt she should have been severely punished, but instead she was sent to the dorm where Miss Craven gave her a bath and clean clothes. After a few hours rest, Miss Wilson sent for her.

Miss Craven ushered her into the headmistress' private office, a now-familiar place where she had often been summoned for "little talks." Miss Wilson sat behind the desk, disappointment etched in her deep-set, gray eyes.

"Well, Ruth, here we are once again. Do you think you'll ever grow out of foolishness?"

Receiving no answer, she went on. "Look at Rachel. Why, she has made a marvelous adjustment to school life. She is a fully assimilated member of our community and will make a fine contribution to society some day. You, my dear, as I have told you many times, have twice the potential of your sister. You could go far if only you would make the effort to work with us.

"Your stubbornness has brought shame and punishment upon you and you have lost your sister, too! We do not discourage family ties here. Many of our pupils have remained close to their siblings, but why on earth would your sister wish to associate with you now? When one family member persists in disobedience, family ties do disintegrate as yours have done. Is this what you want?"

What she said was lies, all of it, Wind Flower thought bitterly. The school did everything it could to sever familial relations. Sisters and brothers were always separated and kept apart no matter whether they conformed to school policy or not. Wind Flower stood silent. There was no use refuting the dorm mistress' words.

"You should know, my dear," the other continued, "the only reason you have escaped severe punishment this time is through the efforts of Hank Landry. Miss Christina was all for confinement and a heavy dose of the whip. I, while inclined to be a bit more lenient, nevertheless favored a long confinement for you. But, Mr. Landry is an old friend. He made a strong plea on your behalf, even foregoing his finder's fee if we acquiesced. Why he should care about a recalcitrant child such as yourself I'll never know, but perhaps he sees in you what I see—tremendous potential.

"Mr. Landry aside, however, I have another reason for leniency in this case. I've recently received some very sad news about your people which I am sorry to have to relay to you. It came through a reliable scout, who had just ridden down from the Tongue River area. There is no easy way to say this, my child. Your entire family, in fact your entire tribe, has been wiped out by a sickness. The old and very young were the first to succumb, but in the end there was no one left alive. I am truly sorry, my dear."

Wind Flower refused to cry. Shaking her head violently, back and forth, willing the other's words away, she refused to believe that all she lived for was gone. Suddenly, there was nowhere to run to, no one to welcome her at her journey's end. In one horrible moment her past had been obliterated, leaving her alone with no one left alive to remember her as she really was, Wind Flower, daughter of the Cheyenne.

"Miss Grayson has already broken the news to Rachel," the other went on. "She took it very well. Your sister is a brave girl. As terrible as this sounds, perhaps this is what you need to finally accept us and this life you are fortunate to have been given. After all, you too would be dead now had you remained with the tribe. Now perhaps you can take a more active part in our community, knowing that we are truly your family—the only family you have left. Why Ruth, you..."

"My name is Wind Flower," she screamed, running from the room, down the corridor and out into the back courtyard. She ran till she reached the chapel, throwing open the door and flinging herself down on one of the benches in the back. Her body heaved with sobs, loneliness and despair washing over her like an icy mountain stream after the winter thaw.

She mourned for several moons, giving herself over to grief, refusing to attend classes, eat meals in the dining hall or sleep in her bed. For the most part the staff left her alone, insisting only that she be in the building at night where she slept on the floor beside the bed, using her scratchy blanket for a sleeping mat.

Several times she attempted to speak to Laughing Dove about their parents, but her sister stared straight ahead, refusing to listen, refusing to even acknowledge her presence. She is no longer Cheyenne, Wind Flower thought. I am the last of the tribe.

In the late summer, not long after Wind Flower had ended her mourning, change came to Rose Academy. Mr. Rose finally gave in to government pressure and sold the school to the Bureau of Indian Affairs. When the government took over, they kept most of the staff on, but Miss Christina Rose resigned shortly after the changeover. Her authority would be greatly diminished under the new regime and her father's declining health demanded that she return home to care for him. No one was sorry to see her go.

There were few that had escaped her cruel lash. Wind Flower wore many scars on her back and legs from the dorm mistress' knotted rawhide whip and although Miss Christina had never again beat her as savagely as that first night, she always watched, waiting for the opportunity to beat down the blue-eyed savage. The beautiful, defiant savage who refused to show fear.

Hatred burned in her eyes whenever she encountered Wind Flower. Hatred of her light skin and fair eyes. Hatred of the tall, slender body growing into beautiful womanhood while her own fat and misshapen figure remained a continual source of amusement and whispered joking among the staff.

Often while helping out in the kitchen, Wind Flower had overheard Cook and Betty laughing about the dorm mistress. Over the years, Miss Christina could not have failed to hear some of their cruel remarks, listening as she did at every keyhole and doorway.

In the fall of 1889, by the white man's calendar, not long after Miss Christina's departure, a new dorm mistress, Catherine Fellows arrived. With her, Miss Fellows brought a group of children from a small government school that had closed to the north of Rose County. With her, Miss Fellows also brought Caleb, changing Wind Flower's life forever and renewing the hope that had died two moons earlier with the news of her family's death.

CHAPTER 13

A crisp fall morning during the Moon When the Deer Paw the Earth (September) heralded Miss Catherine Fellows and her students' arrival at Rose Academy. Classes had been suspended so that the last of the harvest could be gathered and most of the older children, Wind Flower included, had been out in the fields since sunrise digging potatoes.

As the wagon crested the hill, turning into the school's tree-covered drive, field workers stopped to stare at the new arrivals. The trees lining the drive blazed orange, red and yellow. The bright sun filtered through the leaves, bathing the wagon in a magical golden shower, turning its occupants into gilded statues like King Midas, Wind Flower thought, shielding her eyes.

As the wagon drew up closer, slowing down under the cool, blanketing shade of the elms, its occupants took on a more earthly appearance as Wind Flower readjusted her eyes, spying Caleb for the first time. As the overloaded wagon creaked into the narrow front courtyard of the school, he held tight to the reins bringing them to a stop at the front walkway.

He was tall with broad shoulders, his black hair cut short, in the style of the white man. He hopped down helping the younger children out. Must have been just recently captured, she thought with admiration, they could never hold such a brave for long. She smiled, watching his strong arms lifting the children down as if he were picking tufts of prairie grass.

Watching the stranger, her feelings surprised her. Although she had grown into her womanhood during the years of her confinement, Wind Flower had given little thought to the opposite sex. Only a handful of older boys remained at the school. Older boys were much in demand by the local farmers. If strong and healthy, a boy was often forced to cut short his education and go to work as young as twelve or thirteen years of age. Frequently he would move away from school, living in a crude shack supplied by his employer.

The farmers worked the boys hard, paid little and charged high rates for room and board. As the boys sunk deeper and deeper into debt to their employers they were forced to work harder to make up the difference. Although there were kind, considerate Washita, many others worked their boys to death, figuring there was more cheap labor to replace those that fell by the wayside.

The few older boys that remained at the school Academy were of little interest to her. Mostly teachers' pets, they had long since lost the fiery independence to which she still clung. From time to time these boys had made overtures of friendship, but Wind Flower shunned them. But this newcomer...maybe he would be different. Might think like she did. Might feel what a man feels for a woman. Watching Caleb Green in the dusty morning sun, Wind Flower's heart ached with a longing unlike anything she had ever felt before.

In the days following his arrival, she kept her distance, watching Miss Catherine Fellows instead. Miss Catherine was a stern taskmaster, strict, but not cruel like Miss Christina. She gave them long lectures on cleanliness, pronouncing the condition of the dormitory "deplorable."

They were kept busy cleaning and scrubbing until the rooms passed her rigorous inspection. "It's not that I'm picky girls, but as we all know, 'cleanliness is next to godliness' and we all want to be near to our Lord, do we not?"

Miss Catherine was partial to sayings and proverbs and always had one on the tip of her tongue to fit the occasion. Wind Flower marveled at the woman's ability to summon up these clever sayings and as time went by she found herself wondering if Miss Catherine didn't somehow manipulate their lives and lessons to create a stage for her proverbs.

The new dorm mistress, although kinder and more humane than Miss Christina, had one thing in common with her predecessor. Like most of the adults at the school, she would tolerate no reference to the past lives of her pupils. She made this very clear in her lecture the first day, "And I will have no tribal mumbo-jumbo. No ceremonies, no Indian rituals, no speaking another language save English. Is that clear?"

When everyone nodded she continued, "Now I know this is not a problem here at Rose Academy, but I have heard stories. Stories of children allowed to worship both the good Lord and the heathen deities. Children allowed to observe old tribal rituals right alongside holy Christian rites. Blasphemy I call it! Blasphemy pure and simple and I'll not stand for it. If you rejoice, do it as a Christian! If you must mourn, do it in the spirit of Jesus Christ. And let me never hear the heathen tongue upon your lips! Do I make myself clear?"

She gave many lectures along these lines, with slight variations. Always the "Indians" were depicted as dreadful savages, capable of unparalleled cruelty and barbarism. Her tales bore no bearing to reality and Wind Flower often wondered why she spoke such lies. Later she learned that two of Miss Catherine's three brothers had been killed by Blackfeet in retaliation for their part in the massacre along the Marias River in the land Washita called Montana. This fact did not excuse the lies that she told, but it did enable Wind Flower to understand the dorm mistress a little better. She too had lost her family.

One of the first changes brought about by the arrival of Miss Catherine and the government takeover of Rose Academy was the giving of surnames to all students. Caleb and the others came with surnames; the students of Rose Academy had none. They had all used the surname Rose, but now with the coming of Miss Catherine they were to have "proper surnames," from a book the dorm mistress had brought with her.

When it was Wind Flower's turn she stepped up, standing before Miss Catherine, waiting. "Now let me see. You are Ruth, is that correct?

"Hmmm, Ruth would sound nice with a surname that begins with 'B' I believe. What do you say? Ruth Bingham, no, no.... too dowdy. Ruth Bowling? Too dull. Ruth Brown? Too bland for a girl with such lovely, delicate features. Ruth Browning. Yes, I like that. What do you say? Is Ruth Browning acceptable? Come, come girl, speak up. I haven't all day. Will you be Brown or Browning? If you refuse to speak I'll choose for you."

"Browning please, Miss."

"Then Browning it is. I've heard a great deal about you, my dear. We will be seeing a lot of each other I understand. You will not only be a part of my Sunday School class, but you have been recommended by Miss Wilson to be a member of my special literature class this year. Although my duties as dorm mistress keep me busy, I always make time for literature.

"In my class you'll learn about another Browning, by the name of Elizabeth, one of my favorite poets. You may go now Ruth Browning, until later." Dismissing her with a smile, there was nonetheless an implicit warning in her tone. "I've heard about you and there'll be no more nonsense now that I'm in charge," her eyes said as clearly as if she'd spoken aloud.

The dorm mistress appeared to be on fairly intimate terms with Caleb Green and relied on him to perform tasks and run errands. Wind Flower learned that he was a year older, but would attend all of the same classes, including her Sunday School class and the special literature group. The first few weeks, he sat in the back of the room during both Miss Pyle's and Mr. Morgan's classes. He was an excellent student.

Clearly fluent and comfortable with the Washita tongue he had most certainly lived among the Washita for a long time. Always ready with the right answer if called upon, he seldom volunteered, preferring to sit quietly listening. She dared not look around for fear he'd catch her watching him, but Wind Flower frequently daydreamed about him and what she might say should they chance to meet.

This daydreaming often caught her off guard, unprepared when called upon, much to the exasperation of Miss Pyle and Mr. Morgan who had come to depend on her for the correct answer. Inattention was not a problem in Miss Catherine's classes, however, as she kept every student rapt with her spirited reading and calls to "literary discourse." In these classes Wind Flower shone, listening carefully and entering into discussions where her opinions were always well-supported by her reading and rereading of assignments.

In spite of herself, she wanted to show this stern, hard woman that she was up to any challenge she might throw her. Miss Catherine recognized this and as the months went by, she drew Wind Flower out, engaging her mind and heart as no other teacher had done in all her time at Rose Academy.

After class Caleb frequently remained with his mentor. Consequently, they seldom met in the hallways changing classes. In her imagination, Wind Flower conjured up a personality and a history for the mysterious Caleb Green, a personality to suit her hopes and dreams.

In her wild imaginings, Caleb Green became the ally she so desperately needed to realize her dream of escape. Even learning of the death of her family had not dampened her dream. Her people might be lost, but Wind Flower still intended to be free. She intended to go back, to find some of the neighboring tribes. Surely they were not all dead. Surely someone would take her in.

Caleb's background in literature, poetry, mathematics, science and geography reached beyond the knowledge of both Alice and herself who had heretofore been considered the best students in the class. He outshone them both with quiet assurance and little effort.

As time went by, Wind Flower discovered to her dismay that she was not the only girl smitten with Caleb Green. At night she often heard Alice and Mary whispering. "Isn't he handsome, Ruth? Oooh, I'm in love," Mary crooned, giggling and falling on the bed in a swoon.

Like the women in Miss Catherine's poetry, thought Wind Flower with disgust, although she secretly felt like swooning whenever Caleb Green came near her. On the fourth day after his arrival, he had taken the seat beside her in Sunday School and her whole body had turned soft, her knees giving way like prairie grass in a wind storm.

Miss Catherine soon called her back, however, always demanding her students' complete attention. "In addition to my strong literary background," the dorm mistress informed them, I am somewhat of a Biblical scholar. I shall endeavor to impart some of my vast knowledge and holy wisdom to you, but my dear students you must be pure and ready to receive my teachings as Jesus' disciples were. Am I understood on this point?" Miss Catherine was always asking rhetorical questions to which she expected no response. And her students always obliged, sitting mutely, as she continued her sermon.

CHAPTER 14

Wind Flower had often rehearsed what she might say should she ever meet Caleb Green alone, but all her practiced words flew away like the butterflies of midsummer when he finally spoke to her. They were on their way to chapel one morning when a familiar husky voice behind her said, "So, Ruth Browning, are you never going to speak to me?"

Startled, she walked on, frantically trying to recall the clever words she had rehearsed. Her practiced words deserted her, however, and she kept right on walking, not daring to turn around.

"Be a snob then," he whispered, overtaking her as they entered the chapel.

Her face bright red, tears threatening to spill, she made her way to her bench. Mary slid in beside her whispering, "What are you doing? The handsomest, most wonderful boy in the school speaks to you and you just ignore him. Are you crazy?" Noticing her friend's obvious distress, Mary patted her arm, adding, "Don't worry. You'll have another chance. He likes you Ruth, I can tell."

All through her morning classes, Wind Flower heard nothing. Three times Miss Pyle called on her, her exasperation rising each time she caught one of her best pupils daydreaming. Finally, her patience exhausted, she said, "Ruth, I will see you after class."

Glad of the excuse to separate herself from the others, Wind Flower waited, bracing herself for a lecture. "All right, my dear—out with it. What's troubling you? You've been in the clouds all week, but today was simply too much!"

Not knowing what to say, Wind Flower sat mute, her head bowed. "Ruth, dear—believe it or not I am your friend. I'm here to help you! You've done so well and Miss Catherine says that you are a star in her literature class. I'm so proud of you. You are living up to the high expectations that Miss Wilson and all of us have always had for you. But now ... what's wrong my dear?"

Although she knew Miss Pyle to be a sensitive, helpful person, Wind Flower dared not confide in her. She longed to ask her teacher if she'd ever been in love, but held her tongue. "I'm sorry, Miss Pyle. I'll try to be more attentive. There's nothing wrong. Really."

Realizing the futility of pressing further, Miss Pyle sighed, "Very well, my dear. Run along to lunch and I'll see you there. Remember, I'm here if you need me."

As Wind Flower slipped into her place at lunch, she was careful not to glance in the direction of the boys' table.

That afternoon Miss Wilson was called to town and the girls' manners class was canceled, granting the girls an hour's free time, an unexpected holiday in their carefully programmed day. Wind Flower decided to take a walk alone, avoiding her friends who had gathered in the shade of the courtyard. She needed time to think, to sort out her feelings.

Older students were allowed to walk in the surrounding woods provided they stayed on the paths used for Mr. Morgan's nature hikes. All paths were clearly marked and well-worn so there was little danger of going astray or losing oneself in the thick, dense pine woods.

A cool day in early winter, the sun shone through the tree tops lighting the pathways with intermittent showers of winter sunlight. They had been spared the snows that sometimes came during the Big Freezing Moon (December) and the leaves covering the path crunched under her feet as she walked.

She followed a path that meandered alongside Rose Creek, a small, rippling stream that ran through the school grounds and provided most of their drinking water. She couldn't stop thinking about Caleb Green. Her emotions churned and roiled till she could hold them back no more. Flopping down on a rock at the creek's edge, she broke into heaving sobs.

First, she had lost Laughing Dove, then her family. She had lost everything that she had ever loved and now this new love—for love it was—brought nothing but confusion, anger and sadness. Instead of filling the emptiness of her heart, her silent love for Caleb Green made her lonely and miserable.

Gradually her sobs subsided and she began to sing—the song of the doe who had lost her family to the hunter. Singing always lifted her spirits and she began to feel better as she sang the last few lines of the doe's tale.

His hand on her shoulder was so gentle at first, that she thought she might be dreaming, but his words broke the spell. "Are you all right?"

Jumping up, she lost her balance and fell backwards, splashing into the shallow creek, her legs splayed out in front of her. Numbed by the icy water, she glanced up, expecting to see him laughing. Instead she found eyes staring down at her with kindness—not a hint of laughter or teasing in his gaze.

She imagined, for an instant, that she could see beyond the green eyes, into his heart, to a place where she felt safe and protected. The moment passed and Wind Flower suddenly became conscious of how ridiculous she must look, laughing as she struggled up. Only then did he laugh with her, reaching down to take her hand, his strong arms lifting her from the icy stream.

Though they barely spoke a word to each other before heading off in separate directions, from that moment on they were friends. Boys and girls were not allowed to spend time together except during Sunday visiting hours and close friendships were definitely discouraged. Punishment would be severe should they be caught along in the woods, but from that day on, their lives were never completely separate again. They spent many hours together, stealing away whenever an opportunity afforded itself.

Time between classes, canceled activities, and free time for the older students, all afforded precious minutes together. They met in the woods, not far from the spot where she'd fallen into the stream.

To use one of Miss Catherine's favorite expressions, they were "kindred spirits." The real Caleb proved to be quite different than the person of her imagination. He had not been kidnapped, but had spent nearly all his life with the Washita who, according to Miss Catherine, had found him abandoned by his parents when only a tiny baby. He longed for freedom as much as she did, dreaming of the day when he could live on his own instead of under the white man's thumb and by their second meeting they were plotting their escape.

"You must be named," she insisted one day, as they sat by the frozen creek. "You cannot go on without a name."

She wanted the decision to be his and his alone. Since he had not been told from which tribe he had been taken, they had no clues to follow, no family history to guide them. Her heart went out to Caleb as they talked about his name. Her family might now have passed onto the Spirit World, but at least she knew who she was. Caleb had no history, no real past except that given him by his white captors.

Wind Flower did not believe that Caleb had been abandoned. It was never the people's way to abandon their young, especially a strong, healthy boy-child. He had been kidnapped, just as she had, she was sure of it. His story, like so many others, was just one more example of Washita "honesty."

After days of deliberation he decided on a name. Caleb prided himself on his swiftness and stealth so he chose the name Shadow Hawk. In their hidden spot in the woods, they secretly performed his naming ceremony. Ordinarily Cheyenne women had very small roles or were not allowed to participate in naming ceremonies, but Wind Flower guided him through the solemn rite of passage as best she could. After that day, whenever they were alone, she called him Shadow Hawk or simply, Hawk. In her heart, Caleb Green had ceased to exist.

Having lived all his life in captivity, Caleb spoke only the Washita tongue so Wind Flower concentrated on teaching him her language—the Algonquin dialect of the Cheyenne. A fast learner, Shadow Hawk caught on quickly, practicing each word, each gesture, each inflection until her smile told him he had it right.

It was almost unnecessary to teach him the language of the body. The universal language of movement and gesture came quickly and they used the subtle, body language to communicate across the dining hall, during study hall and in the middle of Miss Wilson's boring lectures at Chapel. If they needed to meet, a message could be conveyed in this way, a meeting time arranged without words.

Despite her friendship with Caleb, Wind Flower still missed Laughing Dove. In the first months after Hawk's arrival, she had almost forgotten Rachel, the Washita girl who lived as a stranger beside her, but when her occasional overtures of friendship were rebuffed it brought home to Wind Flower the loneliness of life without her beloved sister. Rachel had become the Washita girl, and wanted nothing to do with a wild, rebellious runaway.

In spite of their estrangement, the shock of Laughing Dove's announcement during Sunday visiting hours, sent her sides reeling.

On that Sunday, Wind Flower sat on the grass chatting with Mary and Alice. It was a warm, sunny day in the time when the horses get fat (early June) and Shadow Hawk had driven Miss Catherine into town so the three girls sat together, speculating on what the approaching summer would bring. Only a week of classes remained and then they would be assigned to summer jobs, cheap labor for surrounding communities. They generally began their jobs the day after classes let out, working until two days before the beginning of the fall semester.

All three of them had worked in the fields the previous summer, picking corn and vegetables. Whatever wage they earned went to the school. Miss Wilson told them the money paid for books and special equipment. At the end of the summer they were each given a dollar, to save or use as spending money.

Wind Flower had saved her dollar to use for her escape. With Hawk's help, she intended to succeed this time. They had decided to wait until the weather turned cold, before attempting the journey. In this way they would have plenty of time to gather supplies. By the Freezing Moon (November) they would be ready.

"Ruth?" She heard the familiar voice from behind, then felt her sister's fingers, lightly resting on her shoulder. Turning, she stared up, shielding her eyes from the sun.

Her voice had changed—it was fuller and richer. Laughing Dove, although still pudgy, had grown taller. Wind Flower's first thought was disgust, at how ridiculous her beautiful sister looked in the Washita ringlets and bows, Miss Annabelle arranged so meticulously in her long, black hair. "I'd like to speak with you a minute please. Alone."

Instantly, Wind Flower rose, reaching to take her sister's hand. Laughing Dove pulled away, rubbing her hands together nervously, as they walked away from the others.

Reaching the side of the building, well out of earshot of the others, Wind Flower turned to her, "What's wrong, my sister? Are you all right?"

"Yes, yes. I'm fine." Her crisp, impatience reminded Wind Flower of Miss Wilson. Despite the intense heat of the day, Wind Flower felt as if icy fingers squeezed at her heart. "It's just I... I have... I have something I think you should know. I'm... I'm... Well—I'm going away this summer, with Miss Annabelle. She's taking me back to Boston with her to visit relatives. She asked if I might go and Miss Wilson gave her permission. So... I just thought you'd want to know."

"Dove, what are you thinking of? It's so far away. You can't—"

"We knew you'd object."

"We? Oh, so now it's we?"

Ignoring the outburst, Laughing Dove continued, her voice strained, "That's why Miss Annabelle suggested that I tell you ahead of time, so you could get used to the idea. I'm going Ruth. It's all settled, so please don't make a fuss. And Ruth, my name is Rachel. Rachel Gray. Please don't use that other again. Why, you could get into a great deal of trouble for saying—"

"Trouble, what do you know about trouble?" Wind Flower cried, wanting to grab her, to shake the Washita curls away.

Despite her reaction, a part of Wind Flower rejoiced, knowing that by taking this trip her sister would be spared a summer of hard labor. Eight-year-olds were considered old enough to work the fields and they were given the most menial tasks. She suspected Miss Annabelle had suggested the trip, in part, to spare her pet from such work. Still she protested, spitting angry words at the stranger standing before her.

"Go ahead—tattle away! Tell them I used your true name! I'm sure it'd earn you all kinds of extra treats from your beloved Miss Annabelle and Miss Wilson. Why not? You don't owe me anything. After all, I was your sister, but now I'm nothing to you. Go ahead, tell her. Tell everyone that the evil Ruth has been using Indian names. Go ahead, you little traitor!"

Her eyes filled up, but Laughing Dove held her chin high, controlling herself. "I am not a traitor, sister. If I was a traitor you would indeed be in trouble. Terrible trouble. Do you think that I don't see your secret language with the boy named Caleb? Do you think I don't see you speaking across the dining hall and during Chapel? What you're doing is strictly forbidden. Even with Miss Christina gone, you'd be beaten and punished severely. But, you are not punished because I hold my tongue. Be careful, my sister, you are playing a dangerous game and soon others may catch you at it!"

With these words, she turned and stalked off, not waiting for a reply. Wind Flower stood watching her retreat, stunned by her sister's words. She had forgotten that Laughing Dove had the eyes of the eagle—the eyes of their mother, keen and observant. Laughing Dove watched and listened when others daydreamed. Her eyes saw what others only guessed at and her older sister was suddenly afraid. Afraid for Shadow Hawk and for herself. Afraid too, for her sister, still small and impressionable despite all her sophisticated airs and haughty talk. Afraid of all the awful things that might happen to her, surrounded by Washita all summer with no one to watch over and protect her.

Returning to the others, she heard Miss Wilson call, "Visiting hours are over children. All in for vespers." Shuffling up the steps, she noticed that the wagon had still not returned. Lucky Hawk, she thought, he'll miss evensong.

She didn't mind the hymns, but the prayers to the Great One, delivered in the booming, unrelenting voice of Miss Wilson, jarred and disturbed the quiet of the late afternoon chapel, leaving no time for silent reflection. Silence was not part of evensong.

Wind Flower wanted to run away that very minute, not sure she could endure another day in the prison that was Rose Academy.

CHAPTER 15

"Did you get your assignment yet?" Hawk asked, as they sat dangling their feet in the cool, shallow water of the creek. Tomorrow classes would let out for summer vacation and all students would be assigned to their summer work placements.

"No, but Miss Wilson wants to see me right after class today. How about you?"

"Cuffeys' store. I'm running errands. It'll be perfect—I get to walk, three miles each way. I'll have lots of freedom to scout around, collect food a little at a time."

Seeing her blank expression, he added, "Supplies! For our escape! By the end of the summer I'll have lots of stuff, if I'm careful."

He was right. It was a tremendous opportunity, a stroke of luck, but Wind Flower stood in stony silence, jealously contemplating the exciting summer that lay ahead for her friend. After two escape attempts, she would almost certainly be assigned to work in the fields again. That way she'd be close to home and they could keep an eye on her. There was no possibility whatsoever that she'd be allowed to work in town and now Hawk was to have all that freedom and be far away from her too.

"Perfect," she replied through gritted teeth, turning away.

"Flower, what's wrong?" He grabbed her hard but she pulled away, running from the woods, feeling foolish, but too angry to stay.

As she sat waiting to see Miss Wilson that afternoon, she pondered the dismal summer lying ahead of her. Soon Hawk would be roaming through town, hearing news of the outside and sneaking supplies for their journey while she would be stuck in the Washita fields, planting, weeding and picking till her fingers bled. From sun-up to sun-down she would toil with nothing to show for it but blisters, scratches and a sore back.

She hadn't the least idea why she'd been summoned to the headmistress' office. Probably wants to get one more lecture in before she goes on vacation, she thought, staring glumly at the closed door. Like many of the teachers, Miss Wilson traveled during the summer months, leaving a skeletal staff to oversee the school. She always appointed an acting head in her absence and this summer, to no one's surprise, she had chosen Miss Catherine to act in her stead.

As she sat sulking, a tall, beanpole of a woman bustled up the hallway, throwing open the office door. "Myra," she shouted and Miss Craven emerged from the inner office. "Myra, I need to see Harriet at once, this very minute!"

"I'm sorry, Mrs. Harrow, but she's very busy today. Can I give her a message for you?"

Ignoring Miss Craven, the woman yelled, "Harriet, you in there?"

The door to the inner office was ajar and Wind Flower heard the headmistress call, "Come in, Mabel." The voice sounded weary and displeased.

The inner door slammed shut and Wind Flower waited for what seemed like hours. Once, Miss Craven emerged, apologizing for the delay and asking her to be patient. "You're so grown up now, you won't miss your rest time, will you Ruth? Dear, please feel free to close your eyes and nap a little on the bench while you wait."

Wind Flower leaned back, closing her eyes, intending to rest for only a minute. Sometime later she was awakened by the sound of voices directly over her. "Looks perfect to me, Harriet.

Just what I'm looking for. Tall, strong and light. Why she'd pass fer one of us easy if dressed up proper."

"I don't know, Mabel. As I told you in the office, I'm just not sure I can—"

"Nonsense. I'll whip her into shape. She'll be so busy with me and the youngins' she'll not have a second to thinka runnin' off. Too soft on 'em, you are Harriet. You know I've always said so. Here girl, wake up." She shook Wind Flower roughly by the shoulder. "There'll be none of that snoozin' when you're with me. Land sakes!"

Wind Flower stood up, embarrassed at being caught unawares. "Ruth, this is Mrs. Harrow. She lives in town. She's looking for a mother's helper for the summer. She has six children and—"

"She's perfect, Harriet. Look at those eyes, blue as the sea! Where'dya find her? Speak up girl. You can talk, can't you?"

"Yes." The same height as Miss Wilson, Mrs. Harrow was considerably thinner, with sharp, angular features. Strands of hair stuck out of her bonnet at odd angles, reminding Wind Flower of a bird, its feathers ruffled after a fight.

Her nose, like the beak of the crow, was sharp and pointed, and her jaw jutted out, hatchet-like from the long, skinny neck. When not speaking her mouth was set in a grimace, lips pressed tightly shut. Her clothes were grays and browns, hanging on her bony frame like loose sacks of grain.

Despite the woman's formidable appearance, Wind Flower had heard the word "town" so she smiled, trying desperately to look responsible.

"All right, Mabel," Miss Wilson said, shaking her head. "I suppose, if you've got your heart set on this...As I said, I have other girls who might be—"

"Nope, I want this one."

"Fine. I'll make the arrangements. I expect she'll be able to walk, but you'll have to release her by seven in the evening. I won't have the students walking home in the dark. Is that clear? In fact, I'd prefer that she stop work in the late afternoon, coming back to school in time for supper so that—"

"Can't be done, Harriet. I need her most at dinner time! My busiest time, land sakes! Need every hand I can git."

"Well, I'm sure that will work out all right. And you will feed her?"

"'Course, she kin eat with the family. Plenty of food with all them young'uns."

"Very well, Mabel. Now, if you don't mind I have—"

"Now, now, no need to git testy, Harriet. I'm going. I'm a busy woman too."

As Mabel Harrow flew out the front door without so much as a good-bye and shaking her head, Miss Wilson ushered Wind Flower into the office.

"Now, Ruth," she began after they were seated. "As you can imagine, I am opposed to this. I have serious concerns about your ability to handle this freedom. I sincerely hope you will not disappoint me and the school."

"No, Miss Wilson."

"Mrs. Harrow will work you hard, but I expect you'll be a big help and fun for her little ones. We can lend you some books to bring with you, to read to them. I'm sure you will be very good with them.

"Now, young lady. I had prepared a long speech to you about your opportunities and your summer plans. Until Mrs. Harrow burst in, I had assigned you to Farmer Oakes' farm. Can I trust you to take this position, or should I send word to Mrs. Harrow that I've reconsidered?"

"No, please Miss Wilson, I'd like to go."

"Very well. After Mrs. Harrow's visit I am way behind here and haven't the time for the lecture I'd prepared, so, off with you. Tell Miss Catherine where you've been and better have Miss Craven write you a note. We'll talk more about Mrs. Harrow later."

Fearful that the headmistress might change her mind, Wind Flower hurried off to find Miss Craven. She didn't care if the Harrow woman beat her every day, she was to work in town! The prospect of the sudden and unexpected freedom filled her with excitement and she almost flew back to the dormitory. Mary and Alice were unimpressed with her news. They both had jobs at school embroidering and sewing and thought the idea of walking into town every day sounded dreadful.

After rest she ran to the woods, waiting impatiently for Shadow Hawk to join her. Even more excited than she herself, he congratulated her over and over and they talked and planned, wondering if they might see each other sometimes as they went about their daily chores.

Actually, things turned out even better than they had imagined. Reluctant to allow her most rebellious pupil to walk to and from the town alone, Miss Wilson required that she be accompanied. "And I'm quite sure that Caleb Green will be a good influence on you, my dear," the headmistress said. "He's a responsible, conscientious boy and very appreciative of the life we have given him. You will listen to him and follow his lead. Perhaps he can teach you a few things!"

Wind Flower answered, "Yes, Miss Wilson," repressing a smile.

Shadow Hawk was right—the summer was perfect. During the long walks their relationship would change, changing them both forever.

CHAPTER 16

During her first days at the Harrows, Wind Flower cried the entire walk home, exhausted and broken from a day filled with Mabel Harrow's unceasing demands. Her employer never struck her, but the constant tongue lashing and tirades over the slightest mistake seemed almost worse than physical punishment. At least a beating was over quickly.

As she stumbled along sobbing, Hawk walked at her side, silent, all his sympathetic overtures brushed aside. The Cuffeys worked him hard, but at the end of the day they shared their table with him in friendship. Kind and considerate, the Cuffeys were quite the opposite of Mabel Harrow.

As they walked into town the pair was often teased, adding to her unhappiness. Another girl from the school, Jane Penwright, had been stoned—chased during an afternoon's sport by a gang of teenage boys. From then on Woody drove her to her job as a mother's helper. Hawk and Wind Flower were allowed to keep walking if they stayed "out of trouble." Eventually, the townspeople grew accustomed to the students' comings and goings and left them alone.

Mabel Harrow believed in getting her money's worth from her help and she never ran out of chores. Wind Flower had been hired to look after the children, but at first she barely caught a glimpse of them. She did all the washing, most of the house cleaning and ran countless errands for the mistress of the house. Mrs. Harrow did all the cooking, but all cleanup chores fell to her "mother's helper."

Wind Flower knew were it not for Miss Wilson, her employer would have kept her far into the night, ironing, sewing and cleaning. "Please, Harriet," Mabel Harrow had pleaded, when Wind Flower first started work, "What can another hour mean to you, or to Ruth? What has she to do here that is more important than helping me get the little ones to bed? Can't we discuss a compromise?"

"Mabel, there is nothing to discuss. You knew the conditions when I agreed to allow Ruth to come to you. I'm sorry but I will not change my mind. Our students' education continues even in the summer months and we need them with us. And, I feel twelve hours of work is quite enough time for a fourteen-year-old girl. I'm quite sure you keep Ruth very busy and while this is admirable, I also feel she needs a few hours to herself. Our students are required to read and study during the summer and Ruth needs her evenings for this purpose."

"Why not allow her to work with us then? She could spend the week nights with us—there'd be time for books every night. Then she could come back to school on the weekends, perhaps on Sundays after services."

"Mabel—"

"That's another thing I was meaning to check with you about, Harriet—Saturdays. Why, I'd sure like to keep her till nine at least, if you—"

"Ruth," Miss Wilson had said, her voice barely above a whisper. "Please go inside."

As Wind Flower walked away, Miss Wilson exploded, "Mabel Harrow, you'll try my patience and someday there'll be no mother's helper available to you. When I think of the state Amy Wills was in two summers ago, after only a month with you, I ... Now you listen to me—Ruth will come for the time agreed upon or no time at all. Is that clear?"

Later that day Wind Flower was called to the headmistress' office. "Come in, Ruth, please. So? How did your first day go?"

"Fine," she lied, hating the job, but wanting desperately to hold on to her freedom. It had been wonderful to walk with Hawk in the early morning, the sun rising slowly in front of them as they talked and laughed. She knew she could endure almost anything if allowed this precious time with him.

"I imagine it was less than fine, but no matter. Mrs. Harrow will work you hard, but she's a good sort underneath. Not really cruel, just a trifle rough around the edges. She's not been given an easy life either, poor soul.

"Now, as you know, I've been very specific in the arrangements for your employment and I wish everyone to stick to them carefully. I will communicate all of this to Miss Catherine, who will be acting headmistress in my absence. If there is any problem, please see her at once. Is this clear?

"Yes, Miss Wilson."

"I don't mean sore fingers or dissatisfaction, my girl. I am referring to your hours. You are expected to be at the Harrows from seven to seven, twelve hours, no more, no less, and this is to be strictly adhered to. You are to leave promptly at seven, no matter what the circumstance, am I clear?" Wind Flower nodded.

"Now, I expect you to work hard and do what the Harrows tell you to do. No nonsense. And you will walk home quickly, no dawdling. I would never have agreed to this were it not for the fact that you will be accompanied by Caleb Green, whom I know to be a responsible, reliable boy. You are to mind what Caleb says on the way home. He is in charge. Do you understand?"

"Yes, Miss Wilson," she replied, smiling through gritted teeth.

"Now off with you. I leave tomorrow and will return in mid-August. I hope you have a productive, useful summer and please keep up with your studies. Your teachers speak very highly of your progress, I would hate to have you falter there. Good-bye, Ruth and good luck."

"Good-bye, Miss Wilson," she said, closing the door behind her, not realizing that her "good-bye" would be the last words she would ever say to Harriet Wilson. After a few weeks, Wind Flower grew accustomed to her employer's demands and the routines that constituted the Harrow's daily lives. Her time in the Washita home offered a welcome change from life at the Academy. She especially enjoyed her time with the children.

While her presence was an adjustment for the older children, the younger ones took to her right away. Her charges ranged in age from Samuel, the eldest, who was nine, to the nine-month-old baby Clementine. In between, there were Rufus, eight, Jamie, five, Sadie Lee, four and chubby little Patty, who was "most three."

The two older boys who had been to school treated her as they saw their friends and elders treat Indians that crossed their path, with cruel taunts and little respect. They either ignored her completely or called her names like "Redskin" and "Squaw." If their mother overheard, she ignored their insolence. What did it matter? She was only a hired girl.

The youngest children more than made up for their older siblings' cruelty, however, bringing her joy and happiness she'd almost forgotten existed after two years at Rose Academy. The school discouraged interaction between older and younger students and her estrangement from Laughing Dove had severed all her contact with younger children. They might be fair haired and pale skinned but the younger Harrows helped to fill the aching loneliness her heart felt with the loss of her little sister.

Their mother, busy with social functions and baking, had little time or patience with them. She loathed their sticky hands clinging to her apron and screamed if they disturbed her while she entertained in the parlor.

Wind Flower wondered how she managed during the rest of the year until an errand boy told her, "Gripes, she ain't never got 'em full time. Hires someone agin every fall. Takes a bit of

interest in the older boys, but the babies ain't fer her. She finds someone fer the winter, then fires 'em come summer sos she kin hire cheap help from the school. Does it every year."

Wind Flower hurried through the housework to have more time to spend with the children. They took long walks, Patty and Clementine in the rickety old buggy, with Sadie Lee and Jamie running alongside helping push. They walked along the outskirts of town, avoiding places where she thought white children might go for fear of taunts or worse, but the few times they encountered Washita children, they let the ragged little band go as if they were invisible. Wind Flower assumed they kept their distance out of fear of Mabel Harrow. At the end of the summer, she discovered the real reason they had not been disturbed. The townspeople believed she was white.

During her second week at the Harrows, she had her first confrontation with the older boys. After sweeping the downstairs, she was headed up to the bedrooms when she glanced out the window. It was a warm, sunny day and she had already washed and hung the bedding out to dry on the clothesline. Peering out the window, she spied muddied sheets lying all over the yard.

Rufus and Samuel had run the entire length of the clothesline, pulling down sheets and blankets and trodding over them. Mrs. Harrow was away at a meeting and the younger children were playing in the enclosed side yard so she called, "Rufus! Samuel! Stop! What are you doing?" The two boys laughed, turning away to continue their sport.

Temper seething, she hurried outside desperately trying to stay calm. "What are you doing?"

"Shut up, Redskin," Samuel yelled. "We're allowed. Now, git outta the way, ya hear? We're havin' fun."

His dark eyes blazed with fire. She thought about Laughing Dove and how implacable she could be when aroused. There would be no reasoning with him. She gazed around at her employer's precious linens and knew Mabel Harrow would punish severely for such an assault on her bed clothes.

"Mr. Waring is just delivering the groceries. Shall I call him over to see this?"

"Shut up, Redskin. You work fer us, remember?"

Stifling the urge to thrash him, she said, "Oh? Well, we'll see. I think if Mr. Waring and I work together on this, you two will have a fair bit of answering to do. I'll go get him," she smiled cheerfully, turning to go.

"Wait," Rufus called. "We didn't mean nothin'. We was only havin' a bit a fun."

"That so. Well now you can both have a bit of fun washing these sheets all over again."

"Now, wait a minute Red—"

"I'll just get Mr. Waring."

"Okay, okay."

She filled the wash tub and the boys worked steadily until the sheets and blankets hung on the line, clean again. When their mother returned several hours later she called from the yard, "Why Ruth, you mustn't of given these sheets a good enough wringing! They're still damp! Ruth! Can you hear me?"

Spying Rufus and Samuel hiding in the bushes of the side yard, she replied, "I'm sorry, Mrs. Harrow. I'll try to do a better job next time."

"Land sakes, I cain't leave for a minute what that somethin's gone wrong! Well, don't just stand there gawking. The children are starving fer their lunch. You make it. I've got to lie down." With that Mrs. Harrow, five months pregnant with number seven, lumbered off to her bedroom, calling down for her mattress. The same mattress she'd wanted left on the porch, "till nightfall, you hear! A good airing, this time for pity sakes!"

For the next few days she saw little of Sam and Rufus. The name calling continued sporadically, but seemed to have lost its feverish intensity. Most times they left her alone.

Unlike their older brothers, Patty and Clementine had been her friends from the start. It had been no work to win them over, so starved were they for affection and love. It took a little longer to draw close to Sadie Lee and Jamie, but soon, they, too, lost their reticence. At Miss Wilson's suggestion, she usually borrowed picture books each day from the school library and read to the children in the afternoons before their nap. Clementine usually fell asleep in her arms as she read and the others nestled around, clamoring to see the pictures. It was a new experience for them. They had never been read to before.

She brought her school readers—with their tales of silly children and beautiful, faraway places and she told them Miss Pyle's stories from Hans Christian

Anderson and the Brothers Grimm—which she had long since committed to memory. She told them Cheyenne tales, thinly disguised as fairy stories, changing the characters from chiefs and warriors into kings and knights. It felt good to recall the stories and to tell them again. Their favorite was an old story similar to the French tale of Cinderella, about the "Rainbow Warrior." She called the warrior into a prince and put all of her heart into the telling. The Harrow children never tired of hearing the "Rainbow Prince" and begged to hear it almost every day.

After reading she sang them to sleep—with a Washita lullaby or a story set to music that she made up as she went along. Like Laughing Dove, the Harrow children loved her croaking songs. And like Laughing Dove, were comforted by the steady and strong voice, even if it was slightly off key.

For these lonely children, a warm presence was a rarity and they clung to her every evening when her departure drew near. This attention was not lost on Mrs. Harrow who continued to resent the school's unyielding stance on the issue, but nonetheless adhered to the seven o'clock time, shooing her out the door.

"See what trouble you cause! Land sakes, I have a time puttin' 'em to bed after you stir 'em all up!" Occasionally after a particularly trying bedtime on the previous evening, Mrs. Harrow would forbid her to be with the children on the following day. "Bad influence. I can see it coming! Stay away from my children and tend to the house," she'd say, piling on extra chores.

The prohibition generally lasted till lunch time when she'd yell, "Ruth. Land sakes, where are you? Don't you know your duties! These children need their lunch! After all, what'd I hire ya fer anyway, you lazy thing? They're attached to you now, for pity sakes! Cain't just abandon them!"

Another member of the household also took notice of the children's growing fondness for her. Samuel Harrow, their father, had been away herding cattle when she first took the job. His journeys across the plains, kept him away for long stretches of time. Town gossip was he came home just long enough to get his wife with child, then took off again.

This time, he returned in mid-summer and stayed nearly three weeks. His presence was not welcomed by his wife or his children. He seemed to frighten them and before the summer was out, he frightened Wind Flower as well.

CHAPTER 17

The Harrow children brought her happiness but Wind Flower lived and breathed for her time with Shadow Hawk. Mostly they talked, but sometimes they'd walk without speaking simply enjoying their precious minutes of freedom. Hawk enjoyed working for the Cuffeys. He loved the independence and drew strength from the work, more determined to escape with each passing day.

Unlike Wind Flower, his errands frequently took him around town. His dark skin guaranteed almost daily taunts and occasional cruel pranks. Boys waited behind the store, tripping him up as he hauled supplies inside. If the Cuffeys caught sight of his tormentors, they ran them off, but they were often too busy to notice. Some nights Wind Flower spied him approaching before he'd caught sight of her. His eyes blackened or face and arms cut and bruised, his whole body sagged in defeat. As soon as he spotted her, his expression changed and he stood taller, but it was too late, she'd seen his pain. She pretended not to notice and his pride kept him from sharing what had happened, but still she worried constantly for his safety.

Three weeks into the summer, they were walking home slower than usual because Mrs. Harrow had released her an hour early. The family was going out for the evening, to a church social, and Mabel Harrow had reluctantly let her go at six rather than seven. Wind Flower had run to Cuffeys, carefully avoiding the main street, and found Hawk sitting on the back stoop, waiting until it was time to meet her.

In her happiness at seeing him, her eyes betrayed her and her love shone for an instant, naked and unashamed. It was only for an instant, but long enough.

"Hello," he called jumping down off the step. Although he acted as if he'd seen nothing, she knew in that one moment she'd opened her heart to him, allowing him to see deep within her. Just as she pretended not to see his pain, he pretended not to have seen but suddenly in that one moment everything had changed.

As they walked, each was acutely aware of the other's presence, unable to speak for fear that a quavering voice might betray them. Over half the way back to school, he suddenly stopped, turning to her. "Flower, I..."

A good five inches taller, he stared down at her then took her in his arms. The love she'd kept hidden for so long was reflected in the dark eyes staring down at her. His eyes mirrored her heart as he drew her to him. Frightened, she slipped away and darted into the woods at the side of the road.

It was a lonely stretch of road, not a farm in sight, and they were still a quarter mile from the perimeter of the school's property. The land around them was uncleared, dense woods bordering either side of the road. Arms and legs scratched by thorns, she ran into the woods, unsure of why she ran, yet powerless to stop herself.

At the edge of a small clearing, he caught up with her. The ground all around was soft and thick with pine needles. "Flower ... what's wrong?" Gently touching her arm, he stepped back as she recoiled. "Oh God, Flower ... I'm sorry."

"I ... Hawk, I can't..."

"Can't what?" His eyes, full of hurt and confusion, gazed down at her.

As their hands touched, she started to speak, but suddenly there was no need for words. As their lips met, they fell into one another's arms and in that moment, Wind Flower found her heart's resting place. A warm, peaceful home where she would always feel safe.

They stood quietly for a long time until the darkening sky made them aware of the lateness of the hour. Hurrying out of the woods, they ran the rest of the way back, but after that day, they were to spend many stolen minutes in that clearing, its floor soft with pine needles. Whispering their love between soft kisses and desperate embraces, they grew closer with each passing day.

If they ran the distance from town to their spot in the woods, they gained precious minutes for their lovemaking and each day they dared to stay a few minutes longer, running that much faster back to school to make up the time. They became bolder on the road as well. When no one was in sight they held hands, occasionally stealing kisses in the fading light of late summer's sun.

CHAPTER 18

In the Drying Grass Moon, towards the end of the Washita month of July, Wind Flower first met Samuel Harrow. Mabel Harrow had taken the four older children to a church picnic and Wind Flower sat in the backyard with Patty and Clementine in the shade of the old elm. Clementine had just woken from her afternoon nap and she lay in Wind Flower's arms, still groggy with sleep.

Her sweet, baby smell mingled with the washing soap of her morning's bath as Wind Flower gently combed her damp hair with her fingers, drying and smoothing it. The infant's chubby hands played with the straps of her school pinafore and Wind Flower leaned down, kissing her soft, pink arm.

"I'll miss you, Clemmie, when the summer's over!" she whispered and was rewarded with a gummy smile. Still placid with sleep, in a moment or two, the baby would be wriggling out of her arms eager to crawl about on the grass.

"What about me?" said a plaintive voice at her side. "Won't you miss me in the fall, Ruthie? Huh?"

"Of course I will, Patty," she smiled, bringing her free arm around to embrace the toddler. "Why, I'll probably miss you more than Clementine! You're my best helper! I'd never have known what to do if you hadn't been here to help me." Kissing the golden curls, matted with sweat, her eyes suddenly filled with tears.

"I love you, Ruthie," he said, squeezing her waist, his short, little arms struggling to reach round her.

"I love you too, Patty," she replied, surreptitiously dabbing her eyes. "Now what shall we do with all this free time? The others'll be gone till nearly suppertime and we have the whole afternoon!"

"I know, let's go fishing!"

"Well ... I don't know. It's so hot and Clementine might be eaten alive by all those bugs down in the swamp. How 'bout something here at home? Stories? Hide and seek? What do you say?"

He sat down hard on the blanket, resting his elbow on his knee, deep in thought. "I know," he cried, but before he had time to tell her, a voice called from the back porch. "Who are you?"

"Papa!" cried Patty, running to the porch, reaching up for a hug. The tall, burly man absently patted his son on the head and brushed by, ignoring the outstretched arms. As he stepped off the porch, she noticed that he walked with a limp, favoring his left leg. Like many white men, Samuel Harrow had a great deal of hair on his face. A scraggly, graying beard hid his jaw and lips and his hair, the same reddish-gold as his four youngest children, was wild and unkempt, sticking up in some spots, matted down with sweat and dirt in others. He was sorely in need of a bath.

His brow was beaded with sweat that he wiped away with a red scarf pulled from the pocket of his pants. His stomach jutted out in front of him, hanging over his belt buckle, giving him a lopsided appearance and he hiked up his arms as he walked presumably to keep his balance.

"Who are you, I said?"

"This is Ruthie, Papa." Patty ran up behind him. "She's takin' care of us this summer. Mama hired her! She's—"

"Hush, son. Let the girl speak for herself."

"My name is Ruth Browning, sir. I'm from the Academy. Mrs. Harrow hired me for the summer as a mother's helper."

"More like a mother's slave, if I know Mabel," he chuckled, looking her over from head to foot. His gaze made Wind Flower uncomfortable.

"Put that baby down and get me a cold drink."

"Of course." Instead of setting Clementine down, she brought the baby into the house, settling her into the crib in the keeping room while she fixed lemonade. Patty followed her into the kitchen, whispering, "Don't mind Papa. He's always a little grouchy when he first gits off of the trail. He'll cheer up in a couple of days."

Their afternoon plans were forgotten as she scurried around doing the master's bidding. First, the bath needed filling, then he wanted coffee and lunch. After that, she unpacked his trail bag full of stinking clothes and threw them on the back porch until she had time to wash them. Finally, he sent her to the saloon for whiskey, scribbling a hasty note for her to take with her, saying, "Give this to whoever answers the door and be quick about it girl. Remember—the rear door, not the front!"

Wind Flower had never dared go near the saloon. The raucous sounds spewing from its open windows frightened her and she was afraid if she ventured too close, a murderous drunk might burst through the swinging doors and strike her dead. Miss Wilson lectured on the "evils of drink" and while she had never elaborated on precisely what form those evils might be, Wind Flower was sure there was evil aplenty in the Red Dog Saloon.

After several knocks the door was opened and a white woman with a painted face and shiny red dress peeked out. Her hair was golden, like Patty's, but unlike his soft, yellow curls, her bright yellow curls sat stiff and unnatural on her head. Despite the painted face and strange appearance, the woman's blue eyes were kind and, summoning all her courage, Wind Flower stepped forward, handing her Samuel Harrow's note.

"Don't worry, honey, I ain't gonna bite ya," she laughed. "Wait here a minute and I'll be right back."

Watchful, Wind Flower's eyes scanned the alleyway, searching for a hiding place should anyone suddenly appear. Before long the painted woman reappeared with a brown bag. "Here you go, honey. Be careful you don't drop it or old Sam'll have your head. You're a pretty little thing. What's your name, hon?"

"Ruth, miss."

"Sally's mine. Sally Waters. Don't believe I've seen you around before. Your folks new in town?"

"No, miss. I live at Rose Academy. I'm working for the Harrows this summer as a mother's helper."

"Poor you! 'Tween that slave drivin' Mabel and her good fer nothing husband, you're not havin' much fun, I'll reckon. Lil 'uns are cute, though, ain't they? I bet they're crazy 'bout you."

"Yes, miss."

"Well, you better run along. Listen here, Ruth, if you ever need any help just ask for old Sally, you hear? I mean that hon. You want me you know where to find me. Understand?" Nodding, Wind Flower ran back to the Harrows, stunned at the white woman's seemingly genuine kindness.

By the time Mrs. Harrow returned with the rest of her brood, her husband had drained the bottle from the saloon. Avoiding the hulking presence glowering at them from the corner of the kitchen, she hastened to set a cold supper on the table. When the blessing had been said, the family ate in silence, all eyes averted from the silent, slurping figure at the head of the table. From time to time Wind Flower caught the children peeking up at him, quickly averting their eyes should his rise up from his heaping plate of food.

Finally, he pushed back his chair and belched, his plate so clean it shone. "Fine bunch a slop to serve a man after near six months on the trail."

"Sam, I'm sorry. We didn't expect you till next week, and—"

"Save yer breath, Mabel. I've heard it all before." With that, he staggered out of the house and headed for the Red Dog Saloon.

As she shoved her out of the house that evening, there were tears in Mabel Harrow's eyes. No wonder she had little kindness left for her children, Wind Flower thought sadly. Married to such a man, kindness must have died a long time ago.

As Patty predicted, Samuel Harrow did cheer up some after a few days at home. Still, he frightened her and Wind Flower kept her distance. Once or twice, he took time to play with his children in the backyard, but mostly he sat in a rocker on the back porch, speaking little except to order food and drink from whomever's ears his bellowing reached. When not in the rocker, he could usually be found at the Red Dog.

Mabel Harrow did not allow drink in the house so Wind Flower was not called upon to make another trip to the saloon. While helping Mrs. Harrow with her errands one day not long after her trip to the Red Dog, she caught sight of Sally. Sally gave her a sly wink.

"Scandalous," her mistress muttered as they passed by. "Dreadful! That filth walking the same streets as decent folk."

CHAPTER 19

Except for the location where Miss Catherine claimed he was found, Hawk knew little about his people. From what she could figure, Wind Flower decided that he most likely came from a small, traveling party of Sioux.

"The Sioux have long been enemies of my people," she explained as they walked home one evening. "So I know little about them. Recently the people have come together to stand against the white soldiers, but living on the reservation, we met few Sioux.

"Once, though, I saw the great chief, Sitting Bull, when he came to meet with our warriors. I remember his eyes, bright, piercing eyes and the way he held himself, his back so straight and proud. By then all the people held him in high esteem. His defeat of the yellow hair, Custer, was a great victory for all Plains people.

"When I was quite small, maybe six or seven, many bands of Cheyenne came together for the Sun Dance and then the warriors went out across the plains to meet with many Ogalala and Dakota Sioux. Perhaps your people were among them."

"I wonder if I'll ever know who my parents were?"

"Do you think Miss Catherine knows?"

"Probably. She brought me to the school when I was a baby. Me and two others."

"And where are they?"

"Both died in infancy. Miss Catherine says that she nursed me back to health, but could do nothing to save the other two."

"Then you must ask her where you came from. Not directly, but slyly. Make her tell you how she nursed you. Maybe she'll let something slip. You know how she loves to talk about herself."

"I don't know. Miss Catherine has been—"

"Never mind," she snapped, walking ahead of him. "It was a stupid idea. Forget it." Miss Catherine, Miss Catherine. It was always Miss Catherine! She was the saint who had rescued him. She had done so much for him! Wind Flower hated Miss Catherine! While she would never have admitted it, she was jealous of Hawk's attachment to the dorm mistress and her jealousy made her ashamed.

They walked the rest of the way in silence, speaking no more of his people. As they neared the school, her heart softened. After all, she thought, even if my people are gone, I have a past, but Hawk has nobody. Besides, she wasn't sure she believed Miss Wilson's story about her parents' sickness anymore. Too many of her fellow students had been told a similar tale. Reaching over as they came through the main gate, she squeezed his hand and hoped he forgave her.

CHAPTER 20

Nearly every day in the hot Washita month of August, Wind Flower and the children went to the river to escape the hot dusty backyard and glowering presence of Samuel Harrow. The older ones swam while Patty waded in, holding Wind Flower's hand, gradually submerging himself, but never letting go as he splashed and spluttered back to the surface. Clementine wore only her diaper and peered down at her brother from Wind Flower's arms, waiting to be splashed.

Then, Wind Flower walked straight into the water, clothes and all and eased down, holding Clementine carefully on her shoulder, the cool water flowing over her. And they'd lie on the grassy bank in the sun 'till their clothes dried before venturing home.

Usually they couldn't get away until after lunch, what with all of her chores and the ceaseless demands of the master. By noon, Mabel Harrow tired of whining toddlers and children under foot, shooed them out the door herself.

Samuel Harrow reminded Wind Flower of a smoldering fire ready to flare up into a roaring blaze if the wind blew just right and she kept her distance, hoping she would not inadvertently provoke him. His relationship with his wife seemed to be characterized by cruelty or indifference and their conversations scared and confused her.

"Do you have to go away again so soon, Sam?" Mabel Harrow asked one evening shortly before supper. "The children barely know who you are and you're away for such a long time."

"Do you want to eat, Mabel? Fer God's sake, do you think I like the trail? I'd just as soon stay here with you all, you know that, but—"

"Would you Sam, would you?"

"Now what exactly is that supposed to mean, woman?" He spit out his words—harsh and bitter, words that chilled Wind Flower's heart.

"Hush. Sam, the children'll hear you!"

"Let'em. Just what are you implying, Mabel?"

"Sam, let go, you're hurting me. I..."

At that moment, Wind Flower tiptoed into the kitchen to fetch the napkins. Spying her, Mrs. Harrow lowered her eyes in shame. She pulled away from him, rubbing her arm. His hand had left angry red marks.

"What're you gawking at, squaw? I don't cotton to help what snoops around. Git out a here before I—"

Not waiting for him to finish, she rushed from the room and out the front door. Skirting the house, she went through the gate to the backyard where the children huddled, waiting for the fight to blow over.

Eventually Mrs. Harrow came out. "Ruth, come on in now, you hear? Finish setting the table." As they worked alongside each other, she whispered, "Please forget what you just saw. Mr. Harrow has not been himself lately. It's this dreadful heat and all."

"Yes, Mrs. Harrow," she answered, grateful that the master had disappeared. Unlike her mistress, Wind Flower hoped with all her heart that the master would depart soon. The sooner the better.

As their father's leaving drew nearer, the children seemed to warm up to him and he to them. In the evening, before supper, Patty often sat on his lap and some afternoons Sadie Lee and Jamie could be found playing checkers with him in the shade of the porch. While the younger ones grew more friendly, Wind Flower noticed that the older boys kept their distance and no amount of coaxing or friendly overtures from Samuel Harrow could draw them closer.

One day, Samuel and Rufus sat bored and cross under the clothesline as their father joked and played with the younger children. "P'rhaps you'd like to play a game with your papa, too?" she said, smiling at the two sulking figures. "You two look like you're up for a game of checkers."

"Leave us be, Ruth," Samuel snarled and Rufus added, "Yeah, leave us be."

The boys had long since given up calling her names and teasing her, but they kept their distance most of the time nonetheless. "No, I won't leave you be. I know two unhappy boys when I see'em and you are the glummest pair I've set eyes on in a long while. Won't you be sad when your Papa leaves and you missed the chance for some fun with him? Go on now—ask him."

"Shut up. Shut up!" Samuel ran at her, pushing her backwards, tearing out of the yard, heading for the river.

"Samuel, what's wrong?" she called, chasing after him.

Trailing behind, Rufus caught up with her at the river's edge. "Go away," Samuel screamed, diving into the water, his arms and legs flailing the water as he swam to the opposite side.

She started to follow, but Rufus held her sleeve, pulling her backwards. "Leave him be, Ruth. He'll be okay. He's just a little touchy about him."

"You mean your father?"

"Taint our father. Taint and we're right glad of it. We was much better off without him, too. Sam and me, we could of taken care of Ma, but he wouldn't leave her be. Took her and us too, then gave her all them babies. Sam and me's forgotten now with all them babies."

"Where is your father, Rufus?"

"Dead. Killed when I was four. He was a good pa, but this one don't care about us. Never has. Told Ma she should give us to the school, 'cause there was too many of us. Told her she'd be better off without us. I heard him. He told her that right after Clemmie was born, last year."

"But your Ma didn't give you up, did she?"

"No, but—"

"So she loves you, and I bet your Papa loved you too. Listen, Rufus, I've gotta get back. Go after Sam and bring him back, will you? Tell him I'm sorry. Okay?"

"Okay," he said softly, giving her hand a tiny squeeze before he jumped into the water.

"Where've you been girl?" Mrs. Harrow called from the kitchen as she came in.

"I'm sorry, Mrs. Harrow. Samuel ran off and I went to fetch him."

"Well, where is he then?"

"He and Rufus are down by the river. They'll be back soon."

"I don't like'em down by the river alone, but it cain't be helped. Come on, I need your help. Mr. Harrow's gone out for a bit, but he'll be wantin' his supper when he gits back. Come on girl, step lively!"

As they worked, Wind Flower said, "Sure was a coincidence that Samuel had the same name as Mr. Harrow. Was that your first husband's name too?" She knew more than likely she'd get slapped for asking such personal questions and she braced herself for her mistress' rebuke.

To her surprise, Mrs. Harrow answered without so much as a "How dare you?" "Twasn't no coincidence. Samuel's name was Frederick. Named after my first husband, he was. I called him Freddy. Of course I wanted to keep the name, but Mr. Harrow wouldn't hear of it. Allowed Rufus to keep his name, but not my Freddy."

"And, who told you Mr. Harrow tweren't my first husband? Oh, never mind, I'm sure there's all kinds of gossipin' goin' on out at that school! Land sakes, they ain't anythin' else to do, all those po' ole spinsters!"

The spinsters are better off than you, Wind Flower thought, boldly continuing the conversation. "Must have been an awful shock losing a husband with two small ones. What happened to the boys' father, was he ill?"

"Murdered. Now hold your tongue, you nosy thing, and git those carrots ready. I'm not about to give those bitties out at the Academy any more fuel for the gossip mill!"

The master did not return for supper. They ate in silence, and she said her goodnights to the family, asking Mrs. Harrow to give her regards to the master who would be departing at dawn. Heading down the lane to the Cuffeys feeling almost giddy at the prospect of life without Samuel Harrow, the gruff voice startled her.

"So the little lady's off work, is she?" He was slumped on a bench in the side alley behind Cuffeys' a half-empty bottle in one hand.

She chose the alley to avoid the town's people and had never met a soul there until now. "Oh, Mr. Harrow..." she spluttered. "We missed you at dinner." He smelled of drink and his eyes, red and ugly, leered back at her.

"Did you now? Well, what a pity! We'll just have to make up for that now, won't we?" Staggering to his feet, he lunged at her, grabbing her by the arm.

"Please, sir, I have to get home. Miss Catherine expects me. She'll worry if I'm late." Struggling proved futile as he only squeezed harder.

"The old spinster won't care if I have me a few extra minutes with her squaw. How 'bout a good-bye kiss?" Drawing her closer, his foul breath gagged her. She kicked and scratched, but he only tightened his grip till she was afraid her arm might break.

"A regular little wildcat, aren't ya?" Laughing, he pulled her along, impervious to the kicks and scratches.

"I know how to tame ya," he snarled, dragging her towards an open barn door midway along the alleyway. "We'll find us a nice little spot fer a bit of fun. That's the only thing you Redskins are good fer, a bit of fun! Get me plenty of darkies out on the trail, but hell—you're practically white. Be near as tasty as the young'uns down at the Red Dog, and free too!"

She tried to scream, but he stuffed his filthy, red scarf in her mouth, covering it with his hand. "Guess we'll have to save the kissin' fer another time. Here we are—old Pete's won't mind if we borrow his barn! All that nice, soft straw, just waitin' fer us. Regular little love nest."

Kicking open the door, he pushed her along in front of him. Desperate to free herself, she sunk her teeth into his arm.

"Why, you filthy little savage!" He struck the side of her head, hurling her to the ground and he threw himself on top of her.

Suffocating under the weight and his foul smell, she continued to struggle, but he was stronger and heavier. Pinned and completely helpless now, Wind Flower knew he'd won. As he tore at her clothes, she closed her eyes, tears of shame and anger streaming down her face. Forcing her mind away from the hurt and degradation of the assault, she prayed it would be over quickly, prayed that he wouldn't kill her after he was through.

Above the sound of his panting, she heard a thud and Samuel Harrow ceased to paw her. His lifeless body still pressed down on her, but he had ceased tearing at her. She squirmed, trying to free herself and his body rolled over to one side.

"Flower, are you all right?" Hawk pulled her up off the floor, his arms circling her trembling body. "It's all right," he whispered, "It's all right."

Finally, stepping back, he surveyed the damage. "Well ... it's not too bad."

"Hawk, I—"

"I know, I know," he whispered, kissing her on the forehead, "but, we have to hurry." Stepping over Samuel Harrow's unconscious body, he led her out the door and they ran down the alley and out on to the road towards school. They raced the first two miles to make up for lost time. Wind Flower's legs shook with weakness and fear, but she pushed on keeping up with him as best she could.

Finally, with a mile to go, he stopped. Looking her over again, he tried to smile, but she saw the worry in his eyes. "Your dress isn't ripped too badly, just the apron straps. And your face. We'll have to stop at the stream and clean you up, but I don't think your bruises will look too bad. You can say you had an accident playing with the children."

"But we have to tell someone, Hawk. We can't just let him—"

"Think about it, Flower. What are they gonna do? Nothing. Besides, who's going to believe you over him? We need to forget it. I don't think I hit him very hard, just a bump. He was pretty drunk. Probably sleep it off and forget all about it. And, you should too. Besides, he's leaving in the morning, come on."

Taking her arm, he bent to kiss her cheek. "It'll be okay." When they reached the stream, he dabbed his handkerchief into the water and gently washed her face and hands. The cool water felt good and she sang softly, soothing herself. Since that first day when he had caught her unawares, Wind Flower had never sung in Hawk's presence, fearing he would laugh at her croaking voice. Now she sang of the soft-eyed doe watching over her fawn. It reminded her of home and the forests around the reservation, where the hunters stalked the deer. The people took only bucks, leaving the does and their young in peace. And, they took only what was needed for food. Unlike the Washita, the people wasted nothing.

Finally, taking her hand, he pulled her to her feet. "My beautiful Flower, your singing is lovely, but we have to go. Promise me you'll sing to me again, all right?"

She smiled, holding his hand as they walked the short distance back to school. Relief at her narrow escape and love for the man who walked beside her, brought unexpected tears that spilled over, streaking down her cheeks. As she wept quietly, Hawk walked beside her, staring straight ahead, pretending not to see.

He had risked everything following Samuel Harrow. Were he caught striking a white man, even Miss Catherine would be unable to save him. Indians, even young ones, were hung for far less serious offenses. There would have been no trial, no jail. The nearest tree would have claimed the man she loved so desperately. Giving each other's hand one final squeeze, they broke apart as they reached the crest of the hill and the school towers came into view.

CHAPTER 21

Despite a hangover and a nasty bump on the head, Samuel Harrow departed on schedule. The entire household heaved a collective sigh of relief at his leaving and no one mentioned his name, no one missed him, not even slightly.

As the summer slipped away, Mrs. Harrow heaped more work than usual on her "mother's helper" knowing that she would soon be gone. "Cain't understand why Harriet won't let me have you a few days longer," she said, as they carried the winter clothes out for an airing. "What's an Indian girl gonna use all that schooling fer anyhow? That Harriet's always had her head in the clouds. Mercy sakes—teaching manners to heathens—what's the sense of that?

"I'm not referring to you, of course dear, but some of those other children. My, oh my! Someone with a firm hand ought to take over and run the place right. Why I could get you children on a program that'd be useful to society and yerselves, 'stead a wastin' all the government's money on high brow learnin'. What do girls need with a lot of literature and mathematics? Much less a bunch of ignorant Indian girls! Boys neither. Workin' with their hands, that's what Indians is good fer. Now I know Harriet gives a little time to cookin' and sewing, but I'm sayin' that's pretty near all ya need. Rest of the time you could be gittin' practical experience workin' in the world in families like ours that need ya!"

Wind Flower listened in silence as her mistress rambled on.

"Now you Ruth, yer a might different like on account of yer nearly white folk yerself. Fact, I can't believe you ain't part white some where's, with that light skin of yers and those blue eyes.

Why with decent clothes, you'd be a right handsome girl. Still got that indian wildness 'round the edges, but we could work on that too.

"Why if I had a few years with ya, I'd tame ya. Drive that wild streak right outta ya. Don't look so surprised—I don't miss much you know. And I know my babies've softened you too. They's mighty fond of you, Ruth. That's another reason I want to keep ya. Doesn't seem quite fair, does it?

"When Harriet gits back I'm aimin' to have a talk with her. P'rhaps she'll change her mind. When's she due back anyhow? Thought it was 'sposed to be weeks ago."

"Miss Catherine says any day now. We haven't had any news in several weeks, but she took the train as far as St. Louis and was coming the rest of the way by coach."

"Lord Almighty, what a trip! Better her than me! All that dust. Harriet's a sturdy bird, though. Land sakes, look at the time. Cain't stand around yapping now. Come on girl, back to work! We's wastin'"

During those final days, she saw little of the children. Mrs. Harrow shooed the younger ones away with threats of a spanking should they "distract Ruth from her duties." She missed her young charges and her heart ached at the prospect of saying good-bye.

During the two months in town, Wind Flower and Hawk had slowly and steadily accumulated supplies. Every penny they earned was saved and hidden along with stolen blankets, tins of food and other supplies that they'd scrounged from school, the store and the Harrow's larder.

They dug a deep trough in the clearing in the woods, lining it with old newspapers and pieces of heavy cloth. Every afternoon on their way home, they'd stash any new supplies in the deep trough, covering it with a trap door made of boards Hawk had pulled from old packing crates. They then covered it with earth and moss and their cache was invisible.

"What else do we need?" she asked, as they sat one evening taking an inventory of their supplies.

"Maps, but I'll get those. I'm going to wait till just before we leave, then sneak the ones we need out of Mr. Morgan's cupboard. He's sure to miss them, but maybe not right away. We study world geography this fall so he won't be using the maps of the Dakotas and Canada."

"Canada?"

"Flower, you have your people; I have no one. If I find no kinsmen, where will I go? This is the only world I know and I never want to return to it. Even if I did, the punishment would be severe. Why Miss Catherine would—"

"My people will welcome you," Wind Flower cried, with an enthusiasm she did not feel. In truth she'd worried a great deal about the reception Hawk would receive in the tribe. Warm and friendly to their own, outsiders often found the Cheyenne distant and unfriendly.

"Flower, you yourself have said many times, Cheyenne don't warm to strangers. How will they greet a man who has spent his whole life as a Washita? And how do we know that there will be anyone left at Tongue River? What if Miss Wilson spoke the truth and they're all gone? We have to plan for—"

"But why Canada?"

"It's a huge country with land enough for us to lose ourselves in. This land is rapidly becoming too small with all the white settlers coming. And, I'm not certain I could ever live on a reservation. From what Mr. Morgan has told us about the Canadian wilderness, I think we could raise our children there with—"

"How can you talk like that? That's the dumbest thing I've ever heard? How can you—you, who has lived all your life, in a cage, know what lies ahead for us? You have no knowledge, no experience! Now you want to move to Canada!"

"You're right, of course," he replied, looking away. "I don't have your experience or your knowledge of what lies ahead for us on the outside. I'm sorry if I've angered you."

"It's late. We should go," she said, kicking leaves over the trap door.

"Flower, wait, I…" His words were lost on her. She ran out of the woods like a deer fleeing the hunter. Away from his talk of Canada, white men, and children.

He had said, "Our children." She knew he spoke wisely and she would stay with him no matter what happened, but children…? She wasn't ready to think about children. They had never even discussed a marriage ceremony, much less children.

At the school gates, she slackened her pace, but Hawk stayed behind. He could've easily overtaken her if he wanted, but he kept his distance. Inside the building they separated without so much as a word as Wind Flower headed for the dormitory.

Halfway up the stairs, Miss Grayson caught her, "Ruth dear, come with me please. All the students are assembled in the chapel. I've been waiting for you and Caleb to return. Don't worry about him," she added. "Mr. Morgan will collect him." The hour was late and she wondered why Miss Grayson hadn't chastised her.

As they made their way across the courtyard towards the chapel, the older woman seemed nervous and edgy. Her mood was infectious and Wind Flower soon found her stomach in knots, fearing some terrible fate awaited them in the chapel. Several teachers stood outside the chapel speaking in hushed tones, their eyes rimmed with tears. They took no notice of her approach. Peering more intently at Miss Grayson, Wind Flower saw that she too had been crying.

When everyone was seated, Miss Catherine rose, her face and demeanor solemn. "Girls and boys, I have called this special chapel service to give you some very sad news. There is no easy way to say this, so I will just come right out with it. Miss Wilson is dead." She paused to let the news sink in.

"Her stage coach was attacked by hostile Indians two days ago. There were three other passengers riding with her and a driver and his assistant. I regret to say that there were no survivors. We've only just gotten the news from soldiers passing through.

"It will take a great deal of time and many prayers before we will recover from this terrible tragedy. It is a tremendous loss to the school and to all. I know you will join with me in sending our prayers to God Almighty on behalf of our beloved Miss Wilson. She can never be replaced.

"This, my dear students, is the life we have rescued you from! Savagery beyond imagination! Let us send our heartfelt thanks to the Lord for saving you from the "heart of darkness" from whence you came." A long silence ensued followed by several scripture readings after which they were dismissed for an early bedtime.

A week of mourning was declared, during which time the students were forbidden to work. When she returned to the Harrows, Wind Flower had less than a week left before the start of fall classes. Mrs. Harrow's pleas to retain Wind Flower into the fall and winter months, fell on deaf ears when she approached Miss Catherine about the matter and she had resigned herself to her imminent loss.

Despite her many lectures and harsh words, Wind Flower found, to her surprise, that she mourned the headmistress. The unexpected feelings of loss upset her and she tried, without success, to shake them off. It was unsettling to find oneself mourning one's jailer and her feelings left her distracted and angry.

During their last week of work, the pair walked home in silence, barely looking at each other. There were no stops along the way to visit the clearing in the woods and no talk of their escape. Their discussion about the future had raised a wall between them neither seemed willing or able to scale. Finally, Hawk broke the silence. "Tomorrow is my last day at Cuffeys'. Flower, we've hardly spoken all week about our plans, but this may be our last chance. Do we need anything else? Can you think of anything?"

"Why ask me?" she snapped. "You've already made up your mind without consulting me. You know better than I what you'll need for your life in Canada." She regretted the words as soon as she'd spoken them, but it was too late. They hung in the air, circling like vultures.

"Come on!" He pulled her off the road into the corn field bordering it. They were far from their hiding spot on an isolated stretch of road, but still she protested. He was taking a terrible chance; Indians were shot for stealing corn. They'd be dead long before they had a chance to explain or identify themselves. Then, they'd probably be shot anyway.

"Let me go."

"Not until you tell me what's wrong. Is it Canada? Is that it?"

"No... I ... I don't know."

"Well what? If you don't want to go to Canada we won't. You know I'll follow you anywhere. Wherever you want. I love you. I was wrong to plan without thinking about you. If it's your wish to live with your people on the reservation, then we will. I'll try—"

"I'm sorry," she cried, throwing her arms around his neck, heedless of the danger. "I'm confused and frightened and there's no one to help us. I've never traveled anywhere alone. Sometimes I feel that I, too, have lived too long with the Washita and that I'll have forgotten the land. That we will fail and be—" He bent down to kiss her softly and they stood, holding each other for what seemed a very long time.

The cart was almost upon them before they heard it. "Shhh," he whispered, and they flattened themselves to the ground, praying the farmer would not glance down the row and spy them in the dirt. Scarcely daring to breathe, they waited until the rumbling of the wheels receded into the distance.

Rising, they hurried home to find Miss Catherine waiting at the door. "Where have you been?" she said, eyeing them with suspicion.

Before she had time to stammer a reply, Hawk spoke up, "Walking home, Miss Catherine. We were late getting started, and—"

"You disappoint me, Caleb. Mr. Barnes just delivered the vegetables and he did not pass you on the Rose County Road! Now, I repeat. Where were you?"

Looking over at Hawk her mind raced, but before he had a chance to speak, she blurted out, "It was my fault, Miss Catherine. I had a terrible stomach pain and had to step off the road a moment to ... And I made Caleb stand guard, just inside the clearing, in case anyone should happen along while I was—"

"Oh for pity's sake, never mind! Inside the both of you! Study is almost over! Oh, and Ruth..."

"Yes, Miss Catherine?"

"Rachel will be returning tomorrow. We've had a letter this morning. She'll be arriving on the early train. I thought you'd want to know."

"Thank you, Miss Catherine."

Laughing Dove! In all the plans and preparations, she'd avoided thinking about her sister. How would she be after three months in white society? Probably more distant than ever, decked out in her frilly dresses, her hair curled and beribboned.

The thought of leaving her sister filled her with sadness, but they had no choice. Laughing Dove would never go of her own free will. If they took her forcibly she would almost certainly give them away and all their careful plans would have been for nothing. No, she would have to return home and let the people—if any remained—decide what was best to do about Laughing Dove.

Chapter 22

Her last day at the Harrows, her mistress was called away to tend a sick friend. The stable boy fetched her early in the morning before Wind Flower's arrival and there had been no time for her mistress to write out a list of chores. A neighbor, Mrs. Albro, had come over to watch the children, but she departed hastily without a word as soon as she spied Wind Flower walking up the drive. Two years earlier, Mrs. Albro's husband had been killed as he led a raid on a Sioux encampment, not far from Rose County. His widow hadn't spoken a word to Wind Flower all summer.

"Ma says to see to the wash and the kitchen," called Patty from the doorway. "but that won't take long, will it, Ruthie? Then we kin go down to the river."

Smiling, she scooped him up, kissing the soft, pudgy cheek and tickling his wriggling body as she set him back down. "A fine idea, Patrick Harrow! We'll do it!"

As she went about her chores, the gentle breeze kept the day's heat at bay. The wash hung out and the dishpan emptied, she quickly packed a picnic and they headed out. Samuel and Rufus carried the blankets and food while Jamie pushed the perambulator—Sadie Lee, Patty and Clementine all scrunched inside.

"Sadie, you is too big fer that buggy," Samuel complained halfway down the drive. "Git outta there and leave some room fer the babies."

"Tain't a baby, Sammie," Patty screamed, his chubby arms wrapped around Clementine.

"Well, if'n you ain't no baby," teased Rufus, "Git out and let Clemmie have some room. You and Sadie Lee's what's known as free loaders."

"Tain't!"

"Tis too!"

"That's enough boys. Sadie Lee and Patty are just fine right where they are. Jamie and I can manage this old buggy just fine, can't we? And Patty's being very gentle with Clemmie. Come on now," Wind Flower coaxed. "Let's not spoil the day with bickering!"

When they reached the river, the squabbling was soon forgotten as they gave themselves over to the beautiful day. Clear, rippling water and the cool shade of the giant trees growing along the bank welcomed them. Time flew as they chased one another in and out of the water, splashing and laughing. Samuel and Rufus held the little ones afloat, patiently letting them swim, including them in their games. Occasionally they'd all retreat to the blanket for a short rest or a bite to eat, visiting with Wind Flower and Clemmie. Then it was back into the water again.

Finally, as the sun inched down behind the trees, she reluctantly called them in. As she packed the basket and loaded up the buggy, Wind Flower glanced over, spying Samuel sitting alone, on a rock at the water's edge, his feet dangling in the water. "Sam, come on!" she called, "I need you!"

He continued to stare down river, pretending not to hear. Rufus was downstream, dragging a reluctant Patty back towards the blanket and Clemmie lay dozing on the blanket. Sadie Lee trudged slowly along the embankment with Jamie holding her hand.

Wind Flower walked over and inched her way onto the rock until she sat beside him. "Sam, is anything wrong?"

"Nope."

"Well then—it's time to go."

"Don't feel like it."

"Samuel, we need to head back. Your ma'll be worried about you. And, besides, I can't manage the babies and the basket without your help."

"Leave me be. I ain't comin'."

Implacable as he seemed, she knew she couldn't leave him. She also knew that if she came home without him, her mistress would send her right back to fetch him and she was afraid she might not find him here when she returned. "Samuel, I'm sorry, but while I'm in charge, you've got to come now."

"Oh shut up, will you! You're leavin' us and you ain't never comin' back, so what do you care what I do?"

"Samuel, that's not true. I do care. I love you all."

"Liar! If you loved us, you'd stay like ma wants you to. You're just like all the rest of 'em. Now, leave me be!"

He jumped off the rock and started swimming towards the opposite bank. Glancing back at Clemmie still sleeping in the shade, she sloshed in after him.

Midway across the shallow ford, she caught up with him, grabbing hold of his arms. He kicked and struggled but she held fast, holding him close to her.

Finally, he gave up fighting and went limp. His arms circled her neck as sobs wracked his skinny frame. "I'm sorry, Ruthie. Sorry for the way we treated you. We was real bad. Don't leave! I've hated all the others 'cept you! They're mean and most of 'em smelly funny too."

"Oh, Sam, I wish I could stay," she cried, holding him as they waded back towards the others. "I'm gonna miss you so much! Maybe the school will let me visit Sundays and when you get a little older you can walk out and see me too!" Her heart ached at the lie she spoke, knowing that if all went well, she'd be far away from Rose County before Samuel would ever be given permission to walk all the way to Rose Academy.

"Will you come again next summer?"

His brown eyes looked up, pleading, and she lied again.

"'Course I will, if your ma'll have me. Now, let's get back now, okay? We don't want to upset the others, all right?" He gazed up at her; she was relieved to glimpse a tiny smile.

The three older children shuffled along, as slowly as possible, knowing good-byes were not far off.

As they finally trudged into the yard, their mother rushed out, waving her arms, "'Bout time you showed up, Ruth Browning! Git those children settled and come in and help me! A whole day wasted! And bring in that wash 'fore it rains!

"Land sakes—yer soakin' wet! Whatever'll you think up next? Git upstairs and put on one of my old house coats! Pity sakes! "Cain't turn my back for an instant!"

The skies were clear, not a cloud in sight, but she knew better than to contradict her mistress. After folding the wash, she hung her damp clothes out to dry and went in to help with supper.

Mabel Harrow was an excellent cook and had prepared a savory broth of sorrel and onions. Sweet and delicious, it reminded Wind Flower of her Na'go's soups, pungent and rich with the plants and roots of the forest.

During the main course, a stew of lamb and vegetables, Mrs. Harrow finally broke the silence. "Well, children. We're to be abandoned again!" Before she could go on, Patty began wailing and Sadie Lee dropped her spoon, sliding off her seat to rush to Wind Flower's side.

"See what you've done," their mother continued, glaring at her. "Another upset, and then off you'll go, leaving me to pick up the pieces. To think of all the time and training I've wasted on you! Land sakes!

"Patty, that'll do! Both of you back to your places at once! I've said my peace—now, let's everyone finish up. We have a special dessert, though pity sakes, I don't know why I bother!"

Surprised, Wind Flower rose to help clear the table. "Sit, Miss Browning. Sammie will do it."

When the dishes were all cleared and everyone seated again, Samuel marched in, holding a cake, glazed with white frosting, its top covered with flowers. One candle burned in its center.

Sugar was very expensive and cakes, rare treats indeed. Sadness forgotten for the moment, they enjoyed every bite of the moist, vanilla layer cake, dubbed "Ruth's desertion cake" by its creator.

After dessert she stayed just long enough to wash up and spend a few minutes with each child. By then it was very late and she knew Caleb would be worried. Finally, she could wait no longer. Changing back into her still-damp clothes, she came downstairs to find her mistress waiting.

"Thank you, Mrs. Harrow. For the cake and for having me this summer. I—"

"Oh land sakes—tweren't nothin'," Mrs. Harrow stammered, grasping her hand in a firm, lingering handshake. "Now, run along and say good-bye to the little ones, quick now. That Miss Fellows'll be after me if'n I keep you late! I hope you'll see fit to come and visit the children. They's gonna miss you!"

"I will. Thank you. Good-bye then."

Hugging all the children and whispering a special good-bye to Samuel, she ran out the door. Caleb waited at the front gate and she turned, waving one last time at the seven figures huddled together. They looked so forlorn standing on the sagging, front porch that Wind Flower felt as if her heart might break. Like its inhabitants, the ramshackle white farmhouse seemed lost and forgotten. Tired and beaten down, it was a lonely fight, a never-ending struggle, to hold on as the rest of the world swirled by.

Wind Flower started running, not stopping until her sides ached and breath refused to come. Only then did she slow down, allowing the tears to come. He took her hand and they walked home in silence, each feeling the wrench of their good-byes.

The Cuffeys had been good to him. They, too, had asked if they might keep him and were he not Miss Catherine's pet, Wind Flower felt sure that the school would have sent him away for good.

Mabel Harrow had been a stern taskmaster but Wind Flower knew that many had worked harder than she had. Some were beaten, others were mistreated or taunted incessantly as they went about their work. Few had made the friends with their employers as Hawk had done and none had grown to love a family of children as she herself had.

Lost in thought, Wind flower forgot about her sister's return until they reached school. Miss Catherine greeted them at the door with a brief lecture about tardiness, then sent them off to evening study. Disappointed that the younger students had already been sent to bed, Wind Flower resigned herself to waiting until breakfast to see Laughing Dove. She expected to be ignored anyway, so there was no real rush. Still, though she dreaded Laughing Dove's cool words and white girl airs, Wind Flower longed to see her beloved sister if only from afar.

"Where have you been?" whispered Mary, as she sat down at one of the study hall's long tables. Shrugging, she looked away, afraid if she spoke she might cry.

Mary would not be put off. She whispered again, "I need to talk to you! Ask to go to the privy."

"No," she hissed. Louder than necessary.

Miss Grayson looked over her spectacles. "Ruth Browning, this is quiet study. This is your final warning."

She glared at her friend and Mary gave up, returning to her book with a loud sigh.

As Wind Flower drifted off to sleep that night, a familiar wail startled her awake. It was a sound she had not heard for almost three years. Before she could rise, Mary was at her side. "That's what I was trying to tell you! It's your sister! It's Rachel!"

"I know who it is," she replied, throwing off the covers. "What's wrong. Is she sick?"

"Not unless you call a broken heart a sickness. The woman who brought her back said she carried on like that all the way across the country. I heard her tellin' Miss Catherine. "Caused an awful ruckus on the train."

"What woman? What are you talking about? Where was Miss Annabelle?"

"That's what I was tryin' to tell you. Miss Annabelle's run off and got married. Left your poor sister stranded with some friends of hers. Just ran off, with some man she met. Eloped they did, in the dead of night, without so much as good-bye.

"Rachel's been crazy with grief. Nothin' seems to help. Guess they've given up and are just gonna let her cry."

More wails echoed in the silence, as Wind Flower pulled on her socks. Stealing out of the room, she tiptoed into the younger girls' dorm.

As Wind Flower slipped in beside her, fresh wails heralded her, "Oh, Ruth. She left me. She just up and left me!"

"Hush," Wind Flower whispered, clapping a hand over her mouth. "I'm here now. It's all right. I'd never leave you. You know that."

"But I loved her," she whispered, her body heaving with sobs. "She was my mother. She promised I would be with her always!"

"I know, little one. I know," she whispered, not sure what to say.

Singing softly, the song of the bear cub alone in the woods, she told of his friends the otter and the badger, who joined him so the cub would not have to walk alone. She sang till Laughing Dove's crying ceased and she slept.

Wind Flower stayed, holding her sister, until early light peeked through the windows, then kissing her sister's cheek, she rose to creep back to her own bed.

At breakfast, she looked over, catching her sister's eye. For a moment Laughing Dove hesitated, confused and conflicted after three years living by Washita rules. Finally, she smiled back, a shy, secret smile that filled her older sister's heart with happiness and hope. She had a sister again!

CHAPTER 23

For the next two moons, during the white man's months of September and October, Wind Flower and Hawk met in the woods behind the chapel whenever they could to plan and organize their supplies. Miss Catherine had reinstituted manners classes, robbing them of that precious hour each afternoon, but they managed to find time between classes and before meals to slip away for a few minutes.

Each night she sang Laughing Dove to sleep, whispering words of comfort, but she did not share their plans. She knew her sister would come, but Wind Flower dared not trust her with their secret, lest Dove inadvertently give them away. Laughing Dove had never been one to keep a secret.

Meanwhile they both scrambled to collect the extra supplies needed for a third person. There was plenty of clothing, but food and blankets must be gathered to accommodate another. Part of each meal was put away, secreted into pocket and pinafore—bread, dried grains and fruits, anything that would keep.

In the school woods, they dug a hole—cruder and shallower than the one in the clearing of the woods off the town road. There they secreted additional supplies when they could slip away. Each trip to the woods was a tremendous risk yet they had to chance it.

With daily checks of students' belongings, nothing was safe in the dorms. Anyone caught with food in the dorm was barred from the dining hall for three days.

Finally, the day came when they were satisfied that their supplies were sufficient. They needed only one more thing—horses. They could take one of the school horses, but Hawk refused to take the other two as they belonged to Miss Catherine. After a great deal of discussion, they decided that the school horse was too slow anyway. They would have to steal horses in town.

Horse stealing was dangerous. If caught they'd most certainly be hung or shot, but they had to have them. Without horses, they would be tracked down and recaptured within a day and all the months of preparation would have been for nothing.

Mr. Morgan's maps would guide them over the plains, back home. Using the colorful charts Hawk had stolen from the geography teacher's closet, Wind Flower traced rivers and towns, following a path that would lead them back to the Rosebud Valley and Tongue River. They estimated the reservation to be a six or seven day ride from Rose Academy and prayed their calculations were accurate. Unless they found food along the way, their provisions would be exhausted after seven days.

What they would find at their journey's end was another matter. If Miss Wilson had spoken the truth, Wind Flower had little to return to along the banks of the Tongue. Still, she wanted to see for herself. If no one remained they would move on.

As the fox flees the wolf, light-footed, swiftly racing over the crunching leaves of the forest floor, Wind Flower's final weeks at Rose Academy flew by. They tried to keep their minds on their studies, but it was difficult and in class Wind Flower found herself constantly daydreaming, rehearsing every step of their escape over and over again.

When not preoccupied with her planning, she began silently wishing her friends good-bye. Good-byes that could never be said, hugs and kisses that could never be given. After three years, Mary and Alice were as close as any girls she had left behind in the tribe and she wished they could come too, though she doubted either girl would wish to go. Alice already dreamed of attending a Washita university, a dream certain to end in disappointment. From what Miss Pyle said, few white girls were allowed to attend universities, never mind an Indian girl from a backwoods country school. Miss Catherine assured Alice she would "pass the examinations with flying colors," but examinations did not guarantee admittance.

Mary wanted nothing more from life than to marry Harry, a former student, now working for a local farmer, and make her living as a seamstress. To live in a shack at the edge of town and have Harry the Crow's babies, those were Mary's dreams. Gentle, kind Mary, with her delicate hands and her beautiful needlework, had never set foot in town. She had no idea of the taunts and jeers that awaited herself and her family. Taunts to haunt their every step for the rest of their lives. The thought of Mary's painful future grieved Wind Flower, but there was nothing she could do. She must leave Mary behind to live her life just as she and Hawk would go on to live theirs.

CHAPTER 24

In the Moon When the Water Begins to Freeze on the Edge of the Streams (October), they made ready for flight. Ample supplies for all three had been gathered and maps carefully studied. Wind Flower and Shadow Hawk felt prepared, excited and anxious to embark on their journey. Wind Flower hoped foraging and hunting along the way would add to their store, keeping them from starvation, should the trip last longer than they anticipated.

Laughing Dove knew nothing. Clinging to her older sister each night, she apologized over and over for her desertion, but Wind Flower kept silent. They had come too far to trust their fate to her sister's mercurial nature. What if Miss Annabelle suddenly appeared, her engagement broken? What if she held out her arms and Laughing Dove rushed right back into them?

The fall progressed as usual. They still had Miss Pyle for English and history and Mr. Morgan for mathematics and geography. Unfortunately, they had begun the fall term with a study of world geography. This study proved frustrating as Wind Flower would have preferred a review of the topography of the Plains states with particular focus on the Dakotas.

She considered asking Mr. Morgan if she might undertake an independent project studying local geography, but decided against it. While he encouraged his students to take on extra research and, in fact, expected at least two "special projects" a year from his more gifted pupils, such a study would seem very strange coming in the midst of their focus on the Mediterranean.

Shakespeare was to be the year-long pursuit of Miss Catherine's special literature group. If Wind Flower had one regret in leaving Rose Academy, it was missing the discussions and readings from the plays and sonnets of William Shakespeare that were to take place during the winter and spring. The plays had been issued to them all at once, their slim, orange covers shiny and new. "They are yours for the year," Miss Catherine had proclaimed as she distributed them as if she were dispensing rare, precious jewels. "You will want to read and reread the plays till their words become part of your soul. They are great gifts, so please take good care of them!"

They began with the histories, reading through the Henry and Richard plays. Richard the Third was Wind Flower's favorite and she read it over and over again, feeling his torment while at the same time repelled by his ruthlessness. After the histories, they began the tragedies. At the time of their escape, they had read 'Macbeth' and 'Hamlet' and were midway through 'the Tragedy of King Lear'.

She was sorry to miss the discussion of 'Lear'. His words like the wild, raging storm on the heath, ravaged her soul, sending icy shivers through her body. Although much of Shakespeare was unfathomable to Wind Flower, the beauty and mystery of the worlds and the characters he created tore into her heart, transporting her to places she could barely imagine.

When packing their belongings, she slipped in eleven of the slim, orange volumes, feeling guilty at the theft, but unwilling to part with them. She took the tragedies of 'Lear', 'Othello', 'Macbeth', and 'Hamlet' as well as 'Richard the Third's five comedies' which the class would read in the spring and a book of sonnets.

Their unfathomable beauty never ceased to draw her in, Shakespeare's words rippling over her like a bubbling creek as it winds down the mountainside. While the society from which they came was hostile and strange, the rhythm and beauty of the stories touched her in a way nothing else in the white man's world ever had.

In Mr. Shakespeare's tales the boundaries of consciousness and unconsciousness blurred and allowed Wind Flower's imagination to soar like the eagle.

Hawk did not share her enthusiasm for Shakespeare and they had many arguments about including the books. "You, who wish to leave the white man behind, now want to burden us with these," he cried. "Why carry his words when we are trying to flee them? You are what Miss Catherine would call a hypocrite!"

Quietly stuffing them into the hiding place, she answered. "I am not a hypocrite, and these are different."

"Different in what way? We need the space for food, Flower. And I'm not going to carry them. Why, I—"

"I'm taking them. I'll carry them. Don't worry!" Turning her back, she stuffed them into the sack. Food for the soul, she thought, but said nothing. He would have only laughed and teased her.

Shadow Hawk did not understand Shakespeare. She often noticed him daydreaming during class discussions and Miss Catherine had caught him unprepared more than once. Wind Flower attributed some of his disinterest to preoccupation with the escape, but she also knew that he did not share her enthusiasm for the "Bard" as Miss Catherine called William Shakespeare.

One afternoon, not long after the argument about the books, he passed her in the hallway whispering their meeting signal as he went by. They'd just come from mathematics class and were headed back to the dormitory for afternoon rest. Miss Catherine had canceled manners class that afternoon to give them extra time to study for her examination the following day.

Usually the tests consisted of ten to twelve quotations from the plays most recently covered. They would be asked to identify the play from which the quotation was taken and explain its meaning, relevance and significance. Miss Catherine was keen on "significance."

After rest, Wind Flower slipped out, heading for the spot in the woods. She dared not stay away long as she would surely be missed if she didn't arrive at study hall within fifteen minutes. Reaching the clearing, she spied him leaning against a tree, skipping stones into the stream.

Remembering the fight over the books, she scowled, angry at his nonchalance considering the risk they took.

"Are you crazy? Miss Pyle has lectured me three times this week for tardiness and Miss Catherine glares at you all through class. You might at least try and look like you're listening in her class, by the way. Now you have me running out here to skip stones when I should be in study hall! If we're caught everything will be ruined!"

Grinning, he stepped around the tree to face her. Each day he grew taller. He towered over her by at least a foot. She wanted to strike his grinning face, but before she had time to move or continue her tirade, he drew her into his arms and kissed her.

It had been a long while since their last kiss. In this spot, so dangerously close to school, they barely even held hands for fear of discovery. Shocked, she pulled away, staring up at him, wondering if he had gone crazy.

"Close your mouth, my lovely flower," he laughed, touching her chin. "Don't worry. I haven't taken leave of my senses. I have something important to tell you. You, my beautiful Cheyenne maiden, are looking at a proud member of the family of Big Foot, chief of the Sioux. What do you think of that?"

"How do you—"

"Miss Catherine. I hinted around last night when she called me in. Don't worry! She suspected nothing! She's in such a state of agitation because her protégé, yours truly, has not taken to the Bard like "that young upstart Ruth Browning.""

"You make her very angry, you know. You are the shining light in her Shakespeare classes and she resents it terribly. Have I told you that she calls you a show-off and—"

"What about your family?" she cut him off, uninterested in Catherine Fellows' opinion of her. Time was slipping away and soon they'd surely be missed.

"Well, after my profuse apologies and avowals of intense admiration for the Bard—"

"Stop calling him the Bard in that mocking way or I'll leave this instant. Get to the point or we will both be caught!"

"Anyway, after my abject display of contrition she invited me in for tea. In our old school we had tea every afternoon together and—"

"That's it. I'm going back." She turned to go, but he grabbed her arm.

"Wait, all right, all right. I'll tell you! Quickly," he smiled, still holding on to her.

Wind Flower stopped struggling and listened.

"Anyway, she started talking about nursing me when I first came to her as a baby. Said I was near death when they found me, abandoned near a white settlement. I let her go on a while, waxing eloquent about her heroic ministrations. Then, I said something like "I wonder what kind of people would do such a thing?""

"Well, that was all she needed. Next thing I knew she was ranting and raving about Big Foot and what savages he and his people were. Said she knew I was a close relative 'cause of the things I had with me. A scout identified blankets and other things that had been left with me. I tried to press her for details, but she shrugged me off. Said all my belongings were burned. But Flower, first she called my people Sioux, then she said that Big Foot and his Minnis—"

"Minneconjou," she said. "You came from the Minneconjou tribe of Sioux. I always thought you were a Dakota. But Minneconjou..."

"I saw the great chief, Big Foot once, but I was too little to remember him. Na'go told me of him though..." her voice trailing off as she remembered, "Many of our people were camped with the Sioux, all banded together after Greasy Grass when the warriors defeated the long Hair."

"You mean General Custer, don't you?"

"Yes, he was killed at Greasy Grass, and many of the Sioux came with our people to Tongue River, to flee the anger of the white soldiers. They were—"

"But Flower," he interrupted. "She said that right now the soldiers are chasing Big Foot across the Plains. She says the Ghost Dance has stirred the Indians into a frenzy and they must be stopped. Do you know what she means?"

"I have never seen the Ghost Dance, but I've heard it. The people wait for a savior—like the white man's Christ. They wait for him to come and bring our warriors back from the dead. To come and rid the land of the white settlers. It is a last, desperate hope. My ni'hu says—"

"Shhh ... Do you hear something?"

Crouching down, they listened. Sure enough, footsteps fell on the path, not far away. They were coming closer. Soundlessly they inched farther into the bush, praying the undergrowth was thick enough to hide them. Scarcely daring to breathe, they knelt, clinging to each other in the damp recesses of the thicket.

Presently, she came into view, and Wind Flower drew in her breath so sharply, she was certain she'd been heard. Pausing in the clearing Miss Catherine glanced over her shoulder, then advanced a little farther and stopped.

So intent had they been in watching Miss Catherine, they had failed to notice the steps of another approaching from the opposite direction until he was almost upon them. Wind Flower jumped up ready to flee, but Hawk held fast to her wrist, clapping his hand over her mouth just as Tobias Morgan brushed past the very bush under which they hid. As they watched, the two greeted each other in a passionate, lingering embrace.

"Oh, Toby," she moaned, "I can't stand it another minute. I shall go mad if we can't be together!"

"Now, now, Cathie. Don't go gettin' all worked up again! These things take time. Grace is not well. I can't leave her just yet, but when she's stronger—"

"Stronger! You've been sayin' that for over a year now and she never gets any stronger! Why if I didn't know any better I'd say she was faking the whole illness to keep you!"

"Now, Cathie, that's unfair. Grace has been sickly for ever so long. Tain't her fault and you know it. "'Sides, there's also the question of employment. We'd have to leave Rose County you know. People 'round here are old-fashioned. They'd never tolerate our getting married and me leavin' poor Grace. We'd never be able to keep our jobs here and you bein' the actin' head and all I don't—"

"Oh, Toby, really! Do you think I give two hoots about this godforsaken place? We could go back East and obtain new positions, and live like civilized people! Decent people! Why, the opportunities are limitless in the East!

"No more Indian brats to watch over, fighting a losing battle to eradicate their horrid upbringing! No more barn raisings on some poor soul's dusty parcel of prairie. How I hate those social events, all the gossip, all the trivial nonsense! And, I long for a proper bath and a night in a fine hotel. Beautiful linens on the beds, flowers on every table. And you and I, together—"

"Soon, my dear Cathie, soon," crooned their geography teacher, as he eased his Cathie to a moss covered spot even nearer to where they crunched scarcely daring to breathe. They watched in horror and fascination as he deftly helped the prim, proper Miss Catherine out of her layers of petticoats and undergarments, until the headmistress of Rose Academy lay not ten yards away from them, naked beneath her lover. As she sat transfixed with embarrassment and awe, Wind Flower wondered absently why he remained almost fully clothes throughout their lovemaking, his dark suit a sharp contrast to the startling, white nakedness of his partner.

She dared not glance at Shadow Hawk whose hand drenched in sweat was still clamped tightly over her mouth. They stayed hidden for a long while after the lovers had departed, the moans and cries of their lovemaking still echoing in the stillness of the darkening woods. When they finally rose neither spoke, each turning to go without hazarding a glance at the other.

It was several weeks before they met alone again and neither mentioned Miss Catherine and Mr. Morgan or the spectacle they had witnessed in the woods. There was nothing to say and they had more important things to discuss. They had set the date for their leaving and there would be no turning back.

CHAPTER 25

After long months of waiting, the night of escape was finally upon them. They had selected Sunday because they had more freedom on Sundays and on Sunday evening Woody went to town.

During visiting hours, they whispered last details to one another. Hawk would go alone to the woods to gather the supplies, while Wind Flower roused Laughing Dove. Then, they would meet outside the front gates of the school, hurrying to the clearing off the town road where their summer stores lay buried. After gathering everything, they would head into town to steal horses.

They knew several barns where horses were stabled. Getting them would be another matter. Wind Flower shuddered when she thought of the horses. Much larger than the people's ponies, the white man's animals scared her. She hadn't ridden in over three years and Hawk had never even sat on a horse. These thoughts, coupled with the knowledge that Laughing Dove was petrified of horses, filled her with dread when she stopped long enough to think. "Everything will be fine," she told herself over and over again. Besides, she had long since decided that even death was preferable to another year under the Washita's thumb.

Waiting until the dorm quieted and those around her slept, she rose and slipped into her traveling clothes. She had taken several shirts and a pair of trousers from the Harrows' rag bag during the summer. Mrs. Harrow hadn't missed them and with patching they suited their needs perfectly. Over the pants and work shirt she slipped her nightgown, in case she was discovered while still in the building.

She had a small pair of knickers and a rough, gray sweater for Laughing Dove. Her short hair would slip easily under a cap, but her sister's would have to be cut. For this purpose, she had stolen scissors from the sewing room. She knew Laughing Dove would put up an awful fuss, but there was no help for it. Search parties would be looking for two girls and a boy, not three boys. Her long, curly locks would have to go.

Gathering her belongings, she slipped out of the dorm room, glancing sadly at her sleeping friends. So many times over the last few weeks she had wanted to tell Mary and Alice good-bye, but always decided against it. It was better for them if they knew nothing.

Reaching her sister's bed, she listened. Soft snores told her that Laughing Dove slept. She'd have to wake her which might be a problem; her sister could be so ornery when aroused from sleep. Patiently, she slipped into the bed. Stroking her sister's hair, she whispered her name in the sweetest voice she could muster, but although Laughing Dove's mouth flexed in a sleepy smile, still she did not wake.

Afraid to stay longer, Wind Flower prepared to carry her sleeping sister out. First, she tied all of their things round her waist, easing back the bedclothes. Marveling how heavy her sister had gotten, she strained to lift her. Finally heaving the sleeping child over her shoulder, she slipped out of the room into the dimly lit corridor. As she wove her way out of the building, Wind Flower prayed that her sister would not awake and start screaming.

Down to the cellar she went, following the same hallways through which they had first entered Rose Academy, finally passing the room with the cold stone floor and buckets of fire water. Many children had come through that room since the sisters' arrival. They often heard the screams of the newest arrivals from their classrooms as they attempted to concentrate on their lessons. Although the routine became more humane after the departure of Miss Christina, the heads of new arrivals were still doused with kerosene, their hair lopped off without warning.

When Woody was out he always left the back door unlocked, Hawk had discovered by accident one evening. She was thankful now. If she'd had to go out a window with her sleeping burden, she'd never have made it. Her shoulders ached, but Wind Flower pressed on till she reached the heavy wooden door. As she pushed it open, its creak echoed through the blackness. She stopped, listening. Silence. She stepped out, leaving the door slightly ajar, instead of chancing another creak. As her feet touched the cold, hard ground, the cool, night air filled her lungs. The moonless sky was clear and covered with stars. She made her way around the building, hugging the brick walls. As the front gate came into view, Wind Flower took a deep breath and started running.

Through the wide, open front courtyard she flew, stopping only when she had reached the shelter of the bushes beside the gates. "Flower," he whispered, from just outside. "Are you all right?"

Too breathless to answer, she slipped through the gates just as her sleeping burden awoke. "Where am I?" Laughing Dove moaned. Her sister sensed a scream was coming and eased her down, clapping a hand over her mouth. "Shhh. Not a sound out of you, little Dove. You're safe. I'm here. You need to trust me and be absolutely quiet. Do you understand?"

She nodded, but still Wind Flower kept her hand firmly over her mouth. "If I take my hand away, do you promise not to speak?" She nodded again. "All right, but remember, you must be very brave and very quiet. We are running away, back to Na'go and Ni'hu. We need your help or we shall all be punished. Understand?"

"Quickly," Hawk said. "We have to hurry."

Following his lead, they ran along the grass at the side of the road. When they reached the clearing, they paused to catch their breath, then loaded up the remainder of the supplies. Wind Flower threw off her nightgown, tossing it into the empty hole.

She then helped Laughing Dove into her clothes, telling her of their plans. At the mention of horses, her sister's eyes grew big as saucers, but she listened quietly without protest until it came time to cut her hair. "I won't let you! No! I don't want short, ugly hair!"

"Now, Little Dove," she whispered, in her sweetest voice. "It's only for a little while and it will grow back in no time."

"I won't! I won't!"

After several minutes, Hawk intervened. "Where are the scissors?"

Without a word, she handed him the shears and he said, "Come here, little one. There's no time to lose."

Laughing Dove opened her mouth to protest, then clapped it shut. Stepping nearer to him, she closed her eyes as his quick, careful snips dispatched the long, dark curls. Tossing them into the hole with the nightgowns, they quickly covered the hiding place with dirt and leaves. Then, pulling the cap he had stolen from the boys' dormitory over her head, he said, "Let's go."

Staying off the road as much as possible, they made their way into town. Only once did someone pass, Woody, returning from his evening in town. As his cart rumbled by, they lay flat in an open field at the edge of the road. If the moon had been full, their escape would most certainly have ended there.

At the outskirts of town, they left Laughing Dove, hidden in the woods with the supplies. Frightened at being left alone, she nevertheless put up a brave front, insisting that she would be fine. "Remember. Not a sound. Don't move from this spot and no one will discover you. Take care, my sister—we will be back soon." Wind Flower and Hawk headed off to the most dangerous part of their journey.

As they crept along in the shadows farther into town, they could hear music and laughter coming from the Red Dog Saloon. The night was still and the sound reverberated along the deserted streets, the white man's raucous laughter muffling the pair's footsteps as they neared the stables. "You stay here and keep watch," he whispered as they entered an alleyway behind the stables. "I'll go in and see what I can find." Nodding, she stepped back into the shadows.

Not long after Hawk disappeared, she heard voices and a group of men entered the alley, heading straight for her. She held her breath, pulling back against the buildings. There was nowhere to run. They had almost passed by when one man paused to light his pipe. "Well, now, what have we got here, boys," he called, holding the match's light up to her face.

Grabbing her arm, he pulled Wind Flower into the light shining from the back windows of the saloon. "Looks like we got us a little thief. Or perhaps this little fella just run out on his family fer a bit a fun in the middle of the night. What 'dya think boys?"

"Yeah, let's take'em to see Sally. Mebbe she'll fix 'im up with a date!" The man who spoke, leaned close to her face. His breath reeked of whiskey, causing Wind Flower's stomach to roll with nausea. "Kinda pretty fer a boy, wouldn't ya say. Don't recognize him neither. How 'bout you fellas? Know him?"

"Cain't hardly see'em in this night. Bring 'em along to Sally's, where we kin get a better look at 'em."

As they dragged her towards the Red Dog, Wind Flower was afraid to struggle for fear that her cap might fall off. She went quietly, waiting for the opportunity to break loose and fearing what Hawk would do if he came upon them.

The ragged band reached the back door of the Red Dog and one man stepped forward, rapping sharply, "Come on Sally, old girl! Open up!" Several minutes later the door was flung open by the woman herself. "What you boys about? It's after hours and this girl needs her sleep."

"Just a minute of yer time, Sally. Got us a young buck lookin' fer a good time." Laughing, he threw his head back, revealing a mouth full of brown and yellow, tobacco-stained teeth. His face was hairy, his clothes stained and rumpled. Turning back to Wind Flower, his face twisted, "Say, don't I know you, boy? Where you from anyway?"

"Up north," she stammered, hoping that would satisfy him.

"Up north, where?"

"Next county."

"What you doin' here, then?"

"Came to visit my cousins. The Harrows."

"That so. Just saw Mabel this mornin' and she din't mention anything 'bout no folks visitin'."

"Now, Smoky," Sally interrupted. "Leave the boy be. I know him. I've even seen him with Mabel walkin' round town."

"You sure?"

"Yes ... And I don't 'spose he's been having much fun with Mabel, do you?" She winked at Smoky.

"Well, 'spose yer right, Sal. P'rhaps we better take him out with us, fer a bit of fun. What dy'ya think?"

The other three laughed and cheered, pulling Wind Flower towards the door. "Just a minute, Smoky," Sally called in a sweet, coaxing voice. "He looks like he's almost of an age. Why not leave him with me? I'll show him a good time and Mabel Harrow'll never be the wiser. Too many people'll spot you fellas with him then there will be hell to pay. You know Mabel, and—"

"P'rhaps you're right, Sal. Me and the boys was headed home anyhow. Here's somethin' fer your trouble," he laughed, tossing some coins on the table. "Come on boys. Let's leave the lovebirds." They left, poking each other, chuckling under their breath.

When she closed the door, locking it behind them, Sally Waters turned and said, "Whatever are you about, girl?"

"Thank you," Wind Flower stammered. Wild with fear for Hawk and what might be happening to him outside, she made a dangerous decision. She decided to trust the painted Washita woman who had protected her from Smoky and the others.

Blurting out their plans as briefly as possible, Wind Flower waited for the woman's reaction. Sally listened, then said, "You'll never git ponies from Tyler's barn. I better go git that friend of yers 'fore it's too late. Stay here. Keep the door locked till I git back." Flying, she returned a short time later, with Hawk in tow.

Once inside, he went straight to her, relief and fear shining in his eyes. "I saw them take you, Flower. I was waiting for the chance to free you. I just didn't think I could—"

"I'm fine, Hawk. There were four of them. There was nothing you could do. And we're safe now, at least for a while."

"Listen you two," Sally interrupted. "We gotta git you outta here 'fore morning or you'll be caught fer sure. Now, lemme think a minute, will ya? Sit down over there and have somethin' to eat. Go on now."

Through a mouthful of bread smothered in gooseberry jam, she asked, "Miss Sally?"

"Yea, hon?"

"How's the Harrow children gettin' on?"

"I cain't rightly say, seein' as how I ain't too friendly with their ma, but I expect they's fine. They's a cute bunch of kids, aren't they? Wish them older two hadda growed up with their real daddy, but Mabel does the best she kin. Don't 'spose life's bin easy with Sam Harrow. Terrible temper, foul mouth, rough hands..." she shivered as she spoke, her expression suddenly looked as if she were in pain.

"Miss Sally?"

"Um," she answered, still distracted.

"What exactly happened to Mrs. Harrow's first husband?"

"Gosh. Thought everybody knew. Sam Harrow shot 'em. Killed him in cold blood he did. Took over Frederick Charles' house, his land and his wife. Made po' little Freddy change his name too. Beat them kids somethin' awful in the beginning he did and I expect he still does on occasion."

"How did he get away with it? Why didn't the sheriff arrest him?"

"Honey, this is Rose County. Folks here are afraid of Sam Harrow. He's real cozy with them Roses and other folks as run things here. 'Fore he done shot Freddy Charles, rumor was he was a courtin' that horrible Christina Rose. 'Course she was throwed over once he latched onto Mabel. Mabel may be hard, but she's a darn sight better than that witch of a daughter old man Rose has got hisself. Even her daddy cain't hardly stand her!

"Sam claimed 'twas Indians that got po' Freddy, but everyone knowed better. Nobody saw him shoot Fred, 'cept Tessie Finley, one of my girls, and she were too scared to tell. Who'd of believed her anyhow?

"Mabel tried to git away from him in the beginning. Took the kids and hid out at the school. But, like I said, Sam Harrow's real thick with the Roses. They got that their headmistress, what was her name?"

"Miss Wilson."

"Yep, that's the one. Old man Rose got yer Miss Wilson to deliver up them kids and Mabel, right straight into Sam Harrow's lovin' arms. They were married that same week and that was that.

"Listen—now—we cain't worry 'bout all that right now," she said, throwing on an old brown shawl. "We gotta git goin. Stuff that fruit in your pockets and follow me. Two horses, is that what yer after?" Wind Flower nodded. "Let's go. Let me do the talkin' if we meet up with anyone, will ya. Up north! Where'd ya get that from?"

Not waiting for an answer, she led them out into the night, away from the Red Dog, running along until they came to a cottage on the outskirts of town. The woods were visible beyond a barn and small horse paddock. "Stay put," she whispered, disappearing into the barn. A short time later, she reappeared, leading a horse and smaller pony, back behind the house towards the river.

When they stood at the edge of the woods she stopped, drawing close. "This here's Dandy, my pony. I've had her since she was born. Gentle as a lamb, and strong. She'll take you wherever you want, believe you me! The other's Goblin, my brother's spare horse. A bit feisty at times, but he's a steady mount. A real work horse, so don't you worry none. If anyone asks, I'll say they's been stolen. I won't need to fake no tears, 'bout Dandy, I'll miss the old girl."

"But why?" she started to ask, then bit back the words.

"Why? 'Cause Sally don't like to see nobody caged up, 'specially children. Godspeed to you both, wherever yer headed. And, stay off the roads—they'll be lookin' fer you."

"Thanks, Miss Sally," they both whispered. There was nothing more to say.

"Now git, the both of you," she said, helping Hawk up onto Goblin's back. Wind Flower knew that he would do better on Dandy, but there was no time to argue. They would switch after reaching Laughing Dove. Turning away, they waved back at Sally Waters, standing alone in the clearing, then tightening her legs, Wind Flower urged Dandy on. With a whinny, the pony galloped off and Goblin followed close behind.

Skirting town, they reached Laughing Dove in a short time and dismounting, they loaded the supplies onto Dandy's back. Then, Wind Flower beckoned to Laughing Dove, "I'll take her. You can carry the packs."

"But, I was to ride—"

"Let's put some distance between us and Rose County, before we argue about this. The yellow horse is a steadier mount." Wind Flower leapt onto Goblin's back, pulling Laughing Dove up beside her. She neglected to mention that she'd seen him holding on to the black horse's mane for dear life, on their brief, gentle ride from Miss Sally's.

After a short distance, she turned back, wondering why he hadn't followed. Riding back, she found the yellow pony standing patiently, enduring his ineffectual attempts to mount her as he flung himself at the saddle. Finally, he gained his seat and grinned sheepishly as Dandy trotted up to meet her.

She had never meant to steal the white man's saddles along with his horses, but as she watched her companion, she was thankful for Dandy's saddle. As they galloped off, he held on to the horn with both hands—the only thing between him and the hard ground of the trail. She decided it would be best to keep both saddles for the time being. Even though her companions would never pass for white children, from a distance, they might sneak by and Washita never rode without saddles.

CHAPTER 26

They rode through the night, Laughing Dove cradled in her sister's arms, using the stars to guide them. They were headed northwest towards the Rosebud Valley and the reservation on the Tongue River. First, they would go to Wind Flower's people, then, depending on what they found, they would continue on in search of Hawk's people.

Wind Flower longed to see her na'gos, her mothers again. Miss Wilson had taught them that "decent people" had only one mother, one na'go, that all others were aunts or cousins. Like so many of her lectures, Wind Flower had listened with only half an ear, quietly keeping to her own beliefs. Why would she want only one mother, when she could have five?

Carefully avoiding the Washita settlements, they traveled slowly. A less circuitous route would have been far too dangerous. Dawn broke as they crossed a deserted stretch of prairie. Tired as they were, they dared not stop on the flat, treeless plain. Pressing the horses forward, they pushed on towards the cover of the woods at the edge of the prairie. The distance was deceptive. What looked to be a short ride took them nearly to midday to reach. Exhausted, they tethered the horses and flopped to the ground, asleep almost immediately.

They awoke under the fiery, red sky of dusk, the sound of hoof beats close by. Together they pulled Laughing Dove with them, drawing farther into the trees.

From their hiding place they watched in horror as a long column of blue coats passed by. Checking the map, Wind Flower

realized that they had veered off of their intended route and strayed dangerously close to Fort Robinson. When night fell they must head east, putting greater distance between them and the soldiers that pounded out of the fort day and night.

Riding through the second night, rested and full from Sally Waters' fruits and bread, the first stirrings of freedom crept over Wind Flower. Except for the men in the alleyway, the escape had gone as they had planned. Without Sally Waters' help, Wind Flower knew they'd, in all likelihood, be back at Rose Academy by now. In solitary confinement. But she wasn't in the cold, dark punishment room after all! She was on the open prairie, riding with the two people she loved most in the world. And, she was going home.

Try as they might, Miss Wilson, Miss Catherine and Miss Christina had not broken her spirit nor her resolve to go home. Aside from the slim, orange volumes of Shakespeare tucked in her saddle bags, she had left Rose Academy and white civilization behind forever. Riding along, under a canopy of stars, her arm around her sleeping sister, Wind Flower felt happier than she had felt since the day of their abduction.

She realized that her companion had left a great deal more behind him than she. Laughing Dove had thoroughly immersed herself in the white culture and customs through her alliance with Miss Annabelle and despite the sisters renewed closeness, she still mourned the loss of her beloved. And she had spent a whole summer in white society, playing with white children, attending their social functions and sleeping in their fancy hotels and houses.

Short of bleaching her skin, Miss Annabelle had affected an almost total transformation of her young, impressionable protégé. The white girl, Rachel, who had frolicked on the manicured lawns of Newport, Rhode Island the past summer, was slowly returning to Laughing Dove, but she would never completely be the same. Wind Flower knew that her sister loved her and looked forward to seeing their family, but a part of her could never let go of the life she had lived with Miss

Annabelle. Wind Flower's heart ached for her wishing she could share the pain, but this was one burden Laughing Dove must carry alone.

And what of Caleb Green, Miss Catherine's star pupil and protégé? His love for her had brought him this far, but Wind Flower sensed an ambivalence, even now, at the path his life had taken. They had not spoken of the lover's tryst they had witnessed in the woods, and she feared to do so. More shocking than the act of love they had witnessed, were the words of his beloved teacher, "No more Indian brats to watch over." They had both heard her words. She may have been a white woman, but she was his only family, thought Wind Flower, and her words must have cut into his heart like a knife.

At the time, Wind Flower had rejoiced, secretly hoping that Miss Catherine's hateful words would strengthen his resolve and help him to break away from her smothering attentions. Now she wasn't so sure. He had mastered his horse, helped out with Laughing Dove and rode staunchly beside her thus far, but she sensed that his broken spirit lay behind, as naked and exposed as his beloved mentor on the mossy forest floor. She wished he would talk to her, share his feelings and his fears, but he spoke little and only when necessary.

After three days, she could stand it no longer. Stopping to rest, they fed the horses, ate a small meal and prepared for sleep. Not wishing to be caught unawares again, Hawk or she had kept watch. As usual, he waited for her to make the decision. Glancing down at his silent, brooding form, anger and frustration welled inside Wind Flower. Turning without a word, she strode out of the clearing.

Stopping a short distance away, she waited, arms folded, her back turned towards their camp.

He came up behind her, lightly touching her shoulder. "Flower, what's wrong?"

Shrugging his hand off, she said, "Nothing."

"Then why are you acting this way? Is this where you will watch today? If so, it's not really the best place to—"

"Don't be stupid," she snapped. "Of course this isn't where I'll watch. I'm not sure I'm ever going to keep watch."

"Then I will, you go and rest."

"Fine!"

"What's wrong?"

"Nothing!"

"Then I'll take this watch. You can take second. Is that what you want?"

"What I want is to talk!" she screamed, unwilling to let him retreat back into his silent suffering. "You ride in silence, you say nothing, you do nothing unless I tell you. What's wrong? You, dare to ask me, what's wrong? Despite what you say, I think you want to be back with Miss Catherine. It is her that you love. You're sorry you came away at all!"

"What are you talking about?"

"You know very well. She raised you, taught you, cared for you!"

"Is that what you think? That I miss Miss Catherine?" Laughing, he tried to grab her arm, but she yanked it away. "Oh, Flower, I'm sorry. Please."

"I'm glad you can laugh! I can see I've made a mistake. I thought I knew you and now I see—"

"Flower," he cried, taking hold of her shoulders, shaking her. "Listen to me. It isn't what you think at all. Yes, I've been quiet the past few days. Yes, I've been upset, but not because I miss Miss Catherine. Don't you give me any credit? I've known her my whole life, you know. Mr. Morgan is not the first man to... Well, anyway. I've never witnessed a scene like we saw in the woods, but there have been others, believe me. Many others.

"Miss Catherine has let her true feelings about her "noble profession" slip many times, believe me. She always wanted to go back east away from all of us savages.

"No, my love, I do not miss our headmistress. My silence and ill humor comes because I'm scared. I'm frightened of everything. I'm frightened about traveling in the dark through this strange country. I'm frightened that we won't find enough food to survive and, most of all, I'm frightened of reaching your tribe and being unwelcome. Flower, I'm scared to death of losing you. I'm not strong like you and I've spent my whole life away from the land. This land that fills you with life, terrifies me. I've ridden beside you these past two days and watched you blossom and change into a person I hardly recognize.

"I'm ready to fight and protect you and Dove and I have no fear for myself, but I'm afraid at our journey's end that I'll lose you, Flower."

He released her, stepping back, his head bowed to hide his eyes that were brimming with tears. Wind Flower put her arms around his neck, her own eyes filling up. "You will never lose me, my brave Shadow Hawk. Not as long as I have breath and strength to come to you. You have my heart and my spirit already. Nothing will ever change that."

"What's going on?" Laughing Dove's petulant voice called out as she crashed through the bushes. They broke apart as she came into view. "Aren't we sleeping here?" she whined.

"Yes, my little Dove, we will sleep," she laughed, hugging her sister as they walked back to camp.

"I'll take the first watch," Hawk said. "You two women have a good rest." He walked behind, but Wind Flower could feel his smile, warm and comforting against her back.

CHAPTER 27

In the Moon Where the Deer Shed Their Horns, during the Washita month of December, they reached the banks of the Tongue. It was daybreak on the sixth day of their journey. For only the second time in their travels, they saw people, not blue-coated soldiers this time, but her own people. Two Cheyenne braves, scouting along the outer boundaries of the reservation, approached them, their horses' hooves clattering loudly over the hard, cold ground of the winter prairie. The early morning sun had not yet warmed the earth and the hollow, empty sound of hoof beats rang out as the riders rode out to meet them.

Wind Flower recognized Spotted Deer and Bear Paw, two boys from the tribe grown into men over the past three years. She called out, galloping towards them, Hawk trailing behind. Throwing off her cap, she waved, crying out the Cheyenne tongue, "We are Wind Flower and Laughing Dove, daughters of Strong Arrow and Smooth Water! We've come home!"

The men leapt from their horses to greet them, peppering questions at her amidst joyful greetings. In the rush of explanation that followed, Hawk was left standing, forgotten until Spotted Deer glanced up at him. "Who's he?" Suspicious eyes studied Shadow Hawk.

She introduced him, speaking in their language as neither Spotted Deer nor Bear Paw spoke English. Regarding the newcomer with distrust and perhaps jealousy, the two braves led them into camp. Following Spotted Deer and Bear

Paw, Wind Flower was conscious of two things. First, she was acutely aware of the woman she had become in her absence. And, second, she realized how isolated Shadow Hawk would most certainly be among her people.

A shy, reserved people, Cheyenne were loving and gentle with their own, but wary and distrustful of strangers. Conservative by nature and in their customs and rituals, Cheyenne were slow to change and slow to accept the new. She realized sadly that Hawk might never feel at home with her people, might always be an outsider. As they approached the tents, she knew she would soon have to leave her family again.

They were led towards a group of tipis at the far end of the encampment. As they passed she wondered at the small number of tipis. What had happened to the rest? It was winter, long past the time of summer migration. There should have been three times the number of tipis. Miss Wilson's words echoed in her mind, "All dead, of sickness." Wind Flower prepared herself for the worse.

Suddenly she spied the familiar hides of her parents' tipi—woven together by Star Blanket's skillful hands. The beautifully crafted dwelling that had provided a warm, watertight resting place against the winter winds. Then Star Blanket appeared at the door of the tipi, her mother's youngest sister, her na'go. Star Blanket, the mother who had always babied and coddled them. Running into her arms, Wind Flower's eyes blurred with tears, her na'go's soft voice whispered her name, comforting and embracing her with love.

"My little Flower and tiny Dove. We thought we'd never see you again. Your father's heart was broken when you disappeared. And look at you," she cried, "All grown into a beautiful woman! But, your hair?"

Laughing, Wind Flower continued to hug her na'go, breathing in her earthy scent. Then, remembering Shadow Hawk, she turned and introduced him. Shyly, he stepped forward to take

Star Blanket's hand, as the other smiled in greeting. Then, in their tongue she asked, "And what of him?"

"There is no him," Wind Flower replied, staring into her na'go's questioning eyes. "There is only us."

"Ah, my daughter, you have grown up. But, things might be difficult for you here. Did you not see Spotted Deer and the way he looked at you? He too has grown up and has not yet taken a wife. There are few women left. Things may prove difficult here for you and your tall, dark Hawk of the shadows."

At the mention of his name, Hawk looked up, waiting for her to translate, but she only shrugged, following Star Blanket into the tent. There were only two sleeping mats in the tipi, a larger one for her and a small one for her child, Leaping Fox, who played in a corner of the tent. He looked up as they entered. Not recognizing the sisters, he lost interest and returned listlessly to his playthings. "Fox, your sisters have come home!" His mother's words had no effect and the boy continued his play as if he were alone.

"Where are the others?" Wind Flower asked, although her heavy heart already knew the answer. Star Blanket and Little Fox were all that remained of her family.

"Gone. All taken with the white man's sickness last year. First, Smooth Water passed on, then your ni'hu. The others followed until Fox and I were alone. The family of Two Claws help us and the government still gives us its rotting food from time to time, but Little Fox has never recovered from the loss of his father. Perhaps with his sisters for companionship, he may..." There was nothing left to say, and Star Blanket's voice trailed off into a whisper.

After three suns, White Deer, the old medicine man, returned. Defying the soldiers' orders to remain on the reservation, he had gone out, as usual, with his assistant to forage for herbs and roots to make his medicines. He greeted them warmly, but in his eyes Wind Flower saw only defeat and despair. His thin frame seemed to barely support him. Frail and slow-moving, White Deer wore the look of one with one foot already standing in the spirit world.

During their remaining days in camp they spent most of their time with White Deer. One of the few survivors who spoke English, he and Wind Flower could converse without excluding Shadow Hawk. He viewed her companion with suspicion, but in deference to her, allowed Hawk inside his tipi, speaking only English in his presence.

White Deer told them of the ordeal of her parents and the terrible sickness that had wasted them away. And he told of the tribe's existence, even worse than it had been three years ago.

"The soldiers have grown hostile since the sickness, Flower. They blame us for becoming ill on the rotting grains and rations they throw at us. The land is barren, nothing will grow on it. They give us cattle, then change their minds and kill all the sickly beasts, keeping the healthy meat for themselves.

"They have slaughtered all the buffalo and shut us up. We are penned like cattle as every year the reservation boundaries grow smaller and the treaties and promises are broken. There's nothing left now. When your father Strong Arrow died, I prayed to be taken with him. Prayed to accompany my oldest friend on his final journey.

"After Smooth Water died, everything that he loved was gone and he just gave up. Your parents mourned the loss of their precious daughters until the day they died. Their spirits were shattered and broken when the searchers finally gave up hope of finding you and they never recovered."

"White Deer," she said, during one of their last talks together. "We cannot stay, Hawk and me. We will travel to find his people and then—"

"It is a dangerous time to walk among the Sioux, my child. The Plains are alive with the Ghost Dance and soldiers are restless and angry. They say Big Foot has fallen ill and has little time left in this world."

"All the more reason for us to find him, soon. Please, wise father, tell us where he is. Please help us."

"No, it's too dangerous and maps or not, you would never find your way without running into blue coats. They are everywhere."

"We will go with or without your help," she said, forgetting that Cheyenne women seldom displayed such defiance.

"Leave me," he sighed. "We have nothing to say."

After a day of silence, White Deer called them to his tent. "Sit," he said as they entered. "I know little of Big Foot's people, but have sent a scout, Tall Crow, to learn their location. The last I heard was in the Moon of Black Cherries (August). At that time they danced on the Good River reservation. If they are there Tall Crow will find them. You will await his return."

"Thank you, father," she said, moving to embrace him.

Brushing her away, White Deer said, "Leave me now, I have work to do." His voice was gruff, but his eyes smiled under the furrowed brow.

Two days later Tall Crow returned. He told them that Big Foot was rumored to be coming down from the Badlands with nearly four hundred of his people, mostly women and children. He traveled with less than a hundred warriors. Some of the people were from Sitting Bull's band, forced to flee when their chief had been killed.

"Wind Flower, hear me well. This is not the time to join with the Sioux. Big Foot is so sick they must carry him and the people that travel with him are starving. It is freezing yet the people

have few hides and tattered tipis. There is little warmth and shelter for these travelers. We suffer here, but not like the Sioux. They are—"

"We will go, White Deer, and soon. If only Shadow Hawk and I go, we'll need little food. We have some supplies still and I haven't forgotten your teachings."

"AHD, my beautiful Flower. You have grown up." Running his hand along a scar on her cheek, a permanent reminder of Miss Christina's lash, he asked, "But you have told us nothing of your life among the Washita. Nothing. And Star Blanket can get little from Laughing Dove."

"It is gone. Like all the pain you have laid to rest, I too have let go. I have brought the dearest part of that time away with me. The only part of the past three years that I wish to remember, and we walk together. I left friends behind and I did so with regret, but that's all there is to tell."

"Tall Crow will go with you," he said, calmly as they rose to go.

"But—"

"He will go with you and guide you to the hills where the Big Foots are camped. The hills that lead to Pine Ridge and Chankpe Opi Wakpala (Wounded Knee). There will be no more talk. I have asked him to go and he will go. I need him to bring back news of our brothers and you must return for your sister. He will bring you back."

And so it was decided. Tall Crow would ride with them to meet the Sioux band. For all her protestations, Wind Flower knew it was best. Tall Crow had a gun—one of the only guns that had not been discovered and confiscated by the soldiers. White Deer had hidden it and a small store of ammunition. These he gave to the scout, delivering the travelers into his care.

As they turned the horses away from Tongue River heading out, snow began to fall. The long, hard journey, destined to end in sorrow, had begun.

A cold shiver passed over Wind Flower with those first snowflakes and it would be many moons before she would feel truly warm again.

CHAPTER 28

It was a bright, winter morning as the three travelers broke camp for the final day of their journey. Before nightfall they would reach Chankpe Opi Wakpala, the creek the Washita called Wounded Knee. It was to this place that White Deer's scouts had assured them Big Foot and his followers were headed. Thus far, the travelers had encountered remarkably mild weather for late in the time of the Big Freezing Moon (December).

As usual, Tall Crow and Shadow Hawk rode ahead and Wind Flower followed behind. Cheyenne women never rode alongside the men. At first, Hawk had hesitated, but sensing her discomfort, he had ridden on ahead taking his place alongside the scout.

Two men could not have been more different, Wind Flower thought, watching the two riders. Shadow Hawk's wide shoulders and strong build were a sharp contrast to the lean, angular frame of the scout, named for the bird he had grown to resemble so closely. Even the pony Tall Crow rode was thin, its spindly legs, extension of its rider. The bodies of man and horse blended into one gaunt, gangly creature, like a thinner cousin of the minotaur from Miss Pyle's mythology stories.

Originally from a neighboring tribe, Crow's people had been forced to march from one barren country to another, till they ended up along the Tongue River. All of his family had perished long ago and he the lone survivor of a once proud family lived alone in a crudely fashioned tipi at the edge of the reservation.

They had been careful not to display affection for each other during the journey, sensing that Tall Crow would take offense. The scout seldom spoke except when he needed to give directions and there had been no idle chatter during the journey.

By midday, they had reached a worn path leading across the hills to Chankpe Opi Wakpala. As she rode behind her companions, Wind Flower found herself wondering where, in the surrounding hills, the parents of Crazy Horse had buried the hearts and bones of their son. Somewhere very close to them, the great Sioux chief, rested in peace after Little Big Man's betrayal at Fort Robinson.

Crazy Horse had gone willingly with his trusted friend, the stories said. Had gone with Little Big Man to meet with the Washita, only to be held by his friend as the white soldier's bayonet thrust forward to end his life. Now, he rested here, in his beloved hills, his grave's location a secret that would die with his parents.

Suddenly, her thoughts were interrupted by a shout from Tall Crow. Looking up she saw his horse rear back as he motioned for them to follow. Obeying without question, they veered sharply off the path. Dismounting, they quickly led the horses into the thicket. The scraggly brush offered scant protection should someone look in their direction but there was nowhere else to hide. Pushing them deeper, Tall Crow stood, watching, cursing in a whisper at his carelessness.

No sooner were they hidden than the sound of hoof beats and the voices of many white men reached their ears. As they watched in horror, blue-coated soldiers filed past, some on horseback, others on foot, and a few wounded carried on stretchers by their comrades.

"They have blood in their eyes," Tall Crow hissed, as several wagon guns rolled by. "I fear what we will find ahead of us." Wind Flower's blood ran cold at his words. She shivered as a cold wind blew, signaling a change in the weather.

They waited a long while after the soldiers passed by. Finally, Tall Crow led them out. "You stay here. I will go alone," he said in English, facing Shadow Hawk for the first time, looking him in the eye.

"No," Hawk replied, his voice somber. "Flower, you can stay if you want, but tell him I'm going." Tall Crow needed no translation.

Shrugging, their guide mounted his horse and waited until they, too, were ready. Dreading what lay ahead, they rode on for several minutes. Climbing a high ridge, they came to the top of a deep gulch. Gazing downward, the carnage surrounded them as far as their eyes could see. Women, children and babies lay all around them. They knew before descending the ridge that they were all dead—their bodies strewn on the cold, hard ground, shot down as they had attempted to flee.

Riding over the next rise, they found more bodies heaped and scattered everywhere. Here, too, they found mostly women and children, a few old men and younger warriors, scattered among them. Many groups appeared to have huddled together for protection, to no avail. They were all dead now, still clinging to one another.

Early on Hawk had leapt from his horse, running from one heap of bodies to the next, searching desperately for signs of life. Tall Crow and Wind Flower watched not wishing to intervene, sickened by the devastation surrounding them. Some of the people had been torn to pieces by the wagon guns, their remains scattered over the bodies of others. As her companions continued to search, Wind Flower rode over the next ridge, away from the dead. There, out of sight of the others, her body heaved with nausea.

After a time Tall Crow spied several Sioux warriors in the distance and rode out to speak with them, leaving her to follow Shadow Hawk in his futile search. Returning shortly, Tall Crow called to her in their tongue, "Wind Flower, we must go. The soldiers may return and the weather is changing. Make him understand. We have to go."

Turning, she looked for Hawk, but he was gone. Riding over the next ridge, she spotted him, pawing through a pile of bodies. "Hawk. We must go! The soldiers—"

"Flower, there's one alive," he cried, still wrestling with the bodies. She watched as he pulled a tiny child from beneath its dead mother. "He's alive! Not a mark on him!" Running back to her, his tiny burden cradled in his arms, she saw that he was right. A young boy, not more than two, clung weakly to his neck.

Hawk gently eased into the saddle, tenderly cradling the child. Incongruously, she found herself marveling at how quickly he had learned to ride. Perhaps, as they rode away from Chankpe Opi Wakpala, if she really concentrated on Shadow Hawk's riding ability, maybe, just maybe, she could hold on to her sanity.

They took the boy, Stone Eyes, to a camp some distance away where they found a few more survivors, among them a woman who had lost her infant. She took Stone Eyes to breast and allowed him to sleep with her. She told them that her baby daughter, just two moons old, had been shot from her arms as she ran. Like Stone Eyes, she too had no family left. Now, at least, they would have each other.

The night was bitterly cold as a blizzard blanketed the hills with snow. Icy winds ripped through the camp, making sleep impossible except for the children who lay nestled inside adults' coats against their skin. Wind Flower held a five-year-old girl whose mother had two others to keep warm. The bones of the tiny, emaciated body, pressed into her, and she wondered how much longer the child would survive her life of starvation and cold.

She has only to step outside of my coat, Wind Flower thought, and the grave awaits her. The spirit world stood with open arms ready and eager to claim her.

They listened to a man named Calf Face, who had been there when the shooting had started. The Sioux had been instructed by the blue coats to give up their weapons in exchange for the soldiers' protection. "We piled our guns and our knives outside of Big Foot's tipi," Calf Face began. "Our chief was very sick, near death, but he wished us to give up our weapons, to protect our women and children from harm. So we did.

"There were soldiers watching from all around. We had no choice with the wagon guns pointing at us. The soldiers were searching all the tipis, tossing our things on the ground and ripping our bedding to shreds in search of weapons.

"Yellow Bird was in the tipi of Big Foot. He refused to give up his gun and a soldier tried to take it. Yellow Bird shot the soldier and then another soldier shot Big Foot. After that the soldiers outside opened fire on everyone. They kept shooting and shooting although we were unarmed and defenseless. They rode over the ridges firing at anyone that moved. The wagon guns went off again and again, killing many with each blast. I managed to pull my wife and daughter to safety, but most were not that lucky."

His eyes lowered and Calf Face spoke no more.

They stayed with the small band for two suns, then headed back towards the Tongue River. Shadow Hawk never inquired about his past and his ancestry. He never asked if Big Foot had a son, kidnapped in infancy. There was no point. The people with whom they traveled were too crazed with grief to recall even two moons ago, never mind eighteen years in the past. Several lifetimes of sorrow and devastation had passed since then, robbing them of their memories. Besides, what was one little child when thousands died with each passing season?

Eighteen years ago Bison had roamed the plains. Now they were a dim memory, along with the life that the Sioux had lived for centuries. A life lived in harmony with the earth, where the people took only what was needed for food, clothing and shelter, leaving the creatures of the plains to graze on the land that belonged to them first, before the coming of man.

The Bison, like their Indian hunters, had gotten in the way of the white man's plans. They allowed the people to be self-sufficient, an idea abhorrent to the Washita who settled for nothing less than total domination. The Bison also took grazing land away from the cattle and sheep of the Washita settlers. They, like their Indian hunters, had to be exterminated.

The three travelers helped repair what was left of the tribe's shelters, ragged piles of worn skins and broken tent poles. They hunted for what scant game could be caught on the frozen, barren land. Then, taking only enough to survive the return journey home, the three left their other provisions and most of their warm clothes with the survivors of Chankpe Opi Wakpala. They urged them to come south with them, but the Sioux declined, as they still hoped to meet up with other survivors that had fled westward.

Bidding them a tearful farewell, the three companions headed homeward. Their nights were spent pressed together against the cold, their days a constant torment of trembling, bitter sorrow. The scant clothing they had left afforded little protection against the extreme cold and icy winds and had they not huddled together to sleep, they would certainly have perished.

Riding through days of numbing cold, Wind Flower often wished she too had died at Chankpe Opi Wakpala so that her heart, like Crazy Horses, might rest in the secret hills surrounding the creek the white men called Wounded Knee. How often she wished, during that horrible ride, for rest and release. Release from a world in which her people and all Indian people, no longer had a place.

Chapter 29

The return journey to the Rosebud Valley and the reservation on the Tongue, was slow going. The ponies, unused to the deep, drifted snow, whinnied continuously, balking at every step. Wind Flower wondered what Sally Waters would say if she could see her precious Dandy, pampered and fussed over, kept in a warm, cozy barn all her life, now struggling to survive the terrible cold, carrying renegade Indians all over the countryside.

When they reached home, Star Blanket welcomed them. Her comforting embrace warmed Wind Flower's heart and she allowed her na'go to lead her into the tipi. Hiding his relief, White Deer chided them for being away too long.

They stayed with her people just long enough to be married. The first four nights of their marriage, they spent in a new tipi, sewn from precious hides stitched by the women of the tribe.

The night before their departure, Wind Flower wrote a letter to Samuel Harrow. She began it "Dear Samuel," then scratched it out and began again:

Dear Freddy,

I hope, if your mother reads this, she will forgive my addressing you so. I, too have been called by a name other than my own and I know, it hurts. I am writing to tell you that I must go away. Far away. I wish I could come and say good-bye to all of you—Rufus, Jamie, Sadie Lee, Patty and little Clementine. I will never forget you.

I could never tell you this, but my real name is Wind Flower, daughter of Smooth Water and Strong Arrow. I am married now. My husband—maybe you remember him? He is the boy who

waited for me every day after work. Then he was known as Caleb Green. He is now Shadow Hawk, son of the Sioux.

I'm sorry I couldn't tell you I was leaving, but we had to keep our plans secret. My sister, Laughing Dove, came with us, too. We are all safe. I wish I could say I'll visit you one day, but where I am going, I can never return. My people are no longer wanted in your land and we must find another. It is not a choice, but the only chance we have to live free, beyond harm.

Kiss all your brothers and sisters for me and remember, you are always in my heart. You will travel with me until the day that I die. I know you will grow up to be a fine man, a kind man and I will look for you in my dreams and my prayers. Take care of your family.

Love,
Ruth (Wind Flower)

She handed the letter to Tall Crow and he nodded, promising to give it to the blue-coated soldiers. With luck, it might reach Rose County and her young friend.

Then, packing their few belongings—including her mother's tool bag, her knife and dibble carefully wrapped in doeskin—they said their good-byes and prepared to set out.

White Deer bent to embrace her, his frail body shivering with cold, "Our hopes go with you, my child. If I were younger, I might venture forth with you. Take care of her Shadow Hawk, son of Big Foot. She is our precious flower and we will sorely miss her."

"I will," Hawk replied, in the Cheyenne tongue.

"Ah, my son," smiled the older man, "You might yet have made a Cheyenne warrior!"

Hugging Laughing Dove for the hundredth time that morning and kissing Star Blanket and Little Fox one last time, Wind Flower mounted Goblin. Laughing Dove wished to stay with Star Blanket. It was the right place for her and her sister did not protest. Still, it was very difficult to turn away from her sister, to lose her again. Bending down, she kissed her forehead one last time, then Wind Flower, daughter of the Cheyenne, galloped away. Away from her people forever.

Tall Crow rode with them for three suns, then he too said good-bye. Speaking in the white man's tongue, he called "Good luck. May the Wise Ones watch over you in your journey and keep you safe."

They rode for many suns, careful to stay far from the roads of the soldiers. Often hungry, always cold and frightened of the unknown that lay ahead, they pressed onward. Finally, in the time of the Dusty Moon (March), they crossed the border into Canada, continuing north until they found a place to camp.

As they pressed on into the vast wilderness that would become their home, Wind Flower sang of the eagle soaring high over the jagged cliffs, its dark wings etched against the infinite blue of the northern sky. As she sang, her heart, like the eagle, lifted up to touch the sky.

Author's Note

In writing SONG OF THE SPIRIT, my first wish was to tell a story—the tale of one girl's courage in a world filled with unspeakable hardship. While I was not trying to "send a message" through Wind Flower's journey, I hope I have given my children and grandchildren a different view of our history.

As a novelist, I love telling a story. As a mother, I wanted to give my children and all children, a story of a courageous, young girl (and boy) as they grew into adulthood.

When I look back at my childhood—almost idyllic in every respect—I cringe with shame at the hours spent viewing such television programs as "Rin Tin Tin" and "Wagon Train," with their horribly false and degrading depictions of North America's native people. The fact that they were allowed to be aired—influencing an entire generation with their heinous lies and slanderous propaganda against the people who truly "belong" on this precious land we revere so highly—is nothing short of criminal.

The Cheyenne were known as the beautiful people, quiet, hard-working, at peace with the earth. While my heroine is a Cheyenne, I knew from the start that I wanted the story to end at Chankpe Opi Wakpala (Wounded Knee) in the year of the massacre, 1890. As I began to research the Cheyenne customs and lifestyle so that I could be accurate in my depiction of their day-to-day existence during that time period, I soon discovered that life, as the Cheyenne had lived it for centuries, had already been destroyed by 1887, when my story opens.

Hundreds, thousands of the beautiful people had already been slaughtered, most of the buffalo were gone, and the Cheyenne had been forced to march from one barren, disease-ridden spot, to another, their children dead or sold into slavery. Those that remained had their horses destroyed, their weapons taken from them, to discourage hunting, making them totally dependent on their white jailers.

I had wanted to set the opening of my story in a "typical Cheyenne encampment." There was no such thing by the late 1880's. By that time, all Cheyenne people lived on government reservations, under the brutal thumbs of their white captors, their land taken from them, their freedom to travel curtailed, their pride trampled over to make way for the onslaught that was Manifest Destiny. In the end, to be somewhat accurate historically, I was forced to place Wind Flower and her family on a reservation, and from there, give them what little dignity I could in the face of such relentless oppression (I gave Tall Crow a horse, for instance, when almost certainly his people's horses would have been destroyed or stolen from them).

This story is a work of fiction, an amalgam of stories and accounts, some a part of history, others from my imagination. Rose County, of course, is fictional, as is the school, Rose Academy. That such schools existed is well-documented in historical records. Not only did the government own and operate such institutions, many others were run by religious groups, occupied in perpetrating their own share of atrocities "in the name of the Lord." Were there any humane institutions? Perhaps. Were there worse places than Rose Academy? Very definitely. Hundreds of Indian children, kidnapped or otherwise, forcibly removed from their families, died at the Carlyle School in Pennsylvania. I chose to depict one reality, not necessarily the worst.

A person who loves a happy ending, my research for SPIRIT left me profoundly saddened, for there is no happy ending for the Native American people. Their world and their lives have been irrevocably destroyed. The one thing I could do, was give my heroine a measure of peace and hope as she moved into adulthood. In reality, had she really lived at that time in history, she probably would have died an early death of disease or starvation.

I love the characters in my books, as if they were my children. I could not destroy Wind Flower in that way. I could not allow her fierce, but gentle spirit to be broken. Her survival is my gift albcit small—as a Washita, to a nation of people with whom my heart and spirit will always lie, in deep and profound apology.

ABOUT THE AUTHOR

M. Lee Prescott is the author of several works of fiction for young adults, as well as resource texts for teachers. Three of her nonfiction titles have been published by Heinemann and she has published numerous articles in the field of literacy education. Lee is a professor of education at Wheaton College in Massachusetts where she teaches literacy related courses for preservice teachers. Her current research focuses on mindfulness and connections to reading and writing, and she regularly visits K-12 schools to teach mindfulness to students. She also teaches abroad, most recently in Singapore.

Lee has lived in southern California Chapel Hill, North Carolina, and various spots in Massachusetts and Rhode Island. Currently, she resides on the river, where she canoes and swims daily. She is the mother of two grown sons, and spends lots of time with them, their beautiful wives and her three extraordinary grandchildren.

Lee loves to hear from readers. Her email is *mleeprescott@gmail.com*.